Mills & Boon Classics

A chance to read and collect some of the best-loved novels from Mills & Boon – the world's largest publisher of romantic fiction.

Every month, four titles by favourite Mills & Boon authors will be re-published in the *Classics* series.

A list of other titles in the *Classics* series can be found at the end of this book.

Rosalind Brett

HOTEL MIRADOR

MILLS & BOON LIMITED
LONDON · TORONTO

ISBN 0 263 72221 X

Made and Printed in Great Britain by
C. Nicholls & Company Ltd
The Philips Park Press, Manchester.

CHAPTER ONE

SOFT-FOOTED Moors in white cotton trousers and shirt, a black cummerbund at the waist and a red fez covering dark oily hair, were clearing the trestle tables from the lawn, carrying away soiled napery and gigantic half-empty dishes, baskets of sweet-meat papers and cigarette butts. A small brown-skinned boy crawled about collecting spent matches and other oddments, and another was diving into the long, spectacularly-tiled pool to retrieve whatever the wind had blown in that direction. By the time it was dark, the formal back gardens of the Hotel Mirador would be as attractively neat as they had been this morning, before outdoor preparations for the Caid's garden party had begun.

Dane Ryland looked down dispassionately from his balcony. The party had been the usual success – a milling throng in djellabahs and turbans, smoking khaki-coloured cigarettes, eating pastries and other sweet concoctions, drinking mint tea but no wine. A few French guests had strolled with the Caid, but there were no women. In their treatment of women, thought Dane, they had something here in Morocco. Not that he disliked the sex; he merely preferred them to stay where they belonged till he had time for them – which was seldom.

He came in from the balcony, sat down at his desk and signed the letters his secretary had placed there. Then he spoke into the inter-com and gave a few instructions. Before he had finished speaking, the small dark secretary had knocked and entered.

"Well, Maynier?" Dane asked. "Was the Caid satisfied?"

"Extremely, monsieur. He added twenty per cent to the cheque for tips. Is it right to give so much?"

"It has to be, if he insisted. But first ask the head waiter to put it to the staff that we'll save the money for them if they wish. They won't wish, of course."

Maynier laughed, and shrugged. "Very well. There are one

5

or two things . . . the Americans in Suite Fourteen are anxious to remain for three more days. I have told them the suite is already promised, but they say they are willing to pay much more to stay where they are."

Dane considered, stroked his lean brown jaw with long bony fingers. "Pierre's better at diplomacy with the guests than I am. What about Suite One?"

"They leave the day after tomorrow. Then it is free for only four days."

"And Seven?"

The little middle-aged Frenchman lifted an expressive eyebrow. "Had you forgotten, monsieur? The woman from England has Suite Seven." He paused pointedly. "She is not very pleased that you have not been able to see her yet. I told her you had been unusually busy with the Caid, but obviously she thought it a poor excuse."

"Lord, I'd forgotten her," said Dane. "About those Americans – tell them I'll probably be able to arrange it in the morning. Send one of the desk clerks up with the bookings."

"And the English girl?"

"Girl?" echoed Dane, fixing the secretary with a grey-green eye. "How old is she?"

"She looks very young – not more than twenty."

"She appeared fairly juvenile in the photograph, but I thought it was faked a bit." He thought for a moment, looked at his watch. "I can give her ten minutes now. Fetch her, will you? By the way, Maynier . . ."

"Yes, monsieur?"

"I'm expecting some sort of message from Monsieur de Chalain. See that I get it as soon as it arrives, will you?"

"Of course." The secretary picked up the signed letters. "I'll bring the English mademoiselle."

Dane nodded, made an entry on his desk pad. Then he half turned and looked across the balcony at the trees which surrounded the garden, and at the square white minaret beside the mosque dome, which rose behind the trees against a deep pansy-blue sky. This was the most familiar picture he knew in

Shiran, because this was the room in which he worked and did his thinking, where he hatched big business with his colleagues and entertained his friends. It was his office and sitting-room and it adjoined his bedroom and bathroom. Dane liked his apartments, but then he liked everything about the Hotel Mirador; its opulence and velvet-smooth running, the sound-less closing of the doors, the excellent food and swift valet service, the quiet, discreet staff. It had taken him four years to transform the old Mirador of twenty rooms and smelly back quarters into the luxury block of rooms and suites it was today. Not bad, particularly as he had handled a good deal of other business as well. He made another note on the desk pad. There came the secretary's familiar tap on the door, his voice saying, "Mademoiselle, you will please enter."

The door closed behind Maynier. Dane stood up, and deliberately looked the girl over. She wore pale pink linen with a white collar, flat white shoes which made her legs look long and brown, and a tiny steel-coloured wrist-watch on a thin wrist. A string-bean of a girl, though her hair was good: bronze, slightly wavy and cut short. Her features were too fine-boned, Dane thought, the blue eyes a shade too intelligent. He didn't trust intelligent women, though this one was too young to have many tricks.

"Miss Yorke?" he said. "I'm Dane Ryland. Sit down, will you?"

She did, and looked at him with candid blue eyes. "Am I being interviewed?"

"Of course not." He sat down himself. "I'm sorry I wasn't able to see you when you arrived."

"That was three hours ago."

"Yes, I know. You were met at the airport all right, weren't you?"

"Thank you, yes."

"I'd have met you myself, but we've had a big day here and I couldn't get away. I did make certain that you'd be met, taken to your rooms and served with a meal. Satisfied with your suite?"

7

A tiny glint came into her eyes; perhaps she had noticed the trace of sarcasm. "It'll do," she said coolly. "I'd like to know what you expect of me."

"That's natural." Dane leaned forward in his chair, with his forearms along the immaculate crease of his off-white linen slacks. "Before you came, I knew exactly what I wanted of you, but now I'm not so sure. How old are you, Miss Yorke?"

"Twenty-one."

"How long is it since you qualified in physiotherapy?"

"Only eight months, but I did lots of practical work during my training, and since then I've been with the Beckmoor Orthopaedic Home."

"You look a bit willowy for such hard work."

"If you have only one patient for me, Mr. Ryland, the next two or three months will be the easiest I've had since I chose my career. I'm as strong as an ox."

"We'll see. You understand what sort of job this is, I suppose?"

"The doctor you contacted in England vetted me very thoroughly before he sent me out." Sally looked about her, at the fine carved desk, the modern Moorish ornamentation of ceiling and walls, the hand-made rugs, the white leather chairs. "Do I work here, in the hotel?"

"Not at first. My cousin couldn't settle here, so I got him into a house on the hillside. It's only a few minutes' walk. Perhaps I should give you some details about him. Cigarette?"

"No, thank you."

He took one for himself from the silver box on the desk. "I daresay the doctor over in England gave you a few details about my cousin. Mike had an accident just under a year ago. He had a zippy little sports car and ran it off the road and into a chasm just outside Shiran, with the result that he had to spend several months in the hospital here. They patched him up very well, but he can't use his left leg. It seems to be almost paralysed from just above the knee down to the toes."

"Quite useless?"

8

"Not quite, or it wouldn't have been much use sending for you. He gets a faint pins-and-needles sensation in the calf and across the foot, and occasionally the muscles ache. The doctor here is sure that with patience and the right treatment Mike could make the leg work again. Trouble is, he's gone defeatist. That's why we couldn't sent him over to England."

"You just want me to put in as much time as I can upon the leg? You realize, of course, that he'd do better in an orthopaedic hospital?"

He said flatly, "If you can persuade him to enter one, I'll buy you a slap-up trousseau when you're ready to get married. So far, it's been like battling with a sick dog."

"If he used to be very active, he feels the inaction more than most people would. Is he willing to co-operate?"

"Ah, that's the point. He doesn't know anything about you."

She stared at him. "You actually got me here without his knowledge? That was risky, wasn't it?"

"Not so very," he said easily. "At the worst I'd only have to pay your expenses and send you back. Actually, I was hoping for someone a little older who might be able to influence him mentally, while plugging away at the physical side of things."

"I see." She was trying very hard to hide her vexation and for that reason sounded over-polite. "You should have worded your advertisement a little differently, Mr. Ryland – made some mention of the fact that you needed someone with a superior brain. Even the doctor you appointed to do the interviewing wasn't aware of that requirement."

Just slightly, he smiled. "You're here, so you may as well have a shot at it. But I want you to go about it in my way."

"What way is that?" she asked coolly.

"Well, he'll have to take to you before he'll let you get busy. I suggest that we go along there together tomorrow morning, and I'll introduce you as someone who's staying at the hotel. Wear your prettiest frock and use all that invalid psychology they must have taught you while you were training."

"It sounds a little odd. Surely he's anxious to have the use of his leg?"

"He's anxious, all right, but he doesn't believe it's possible. If you can convince him, you'll have done a wonderful job without using your hands."

She asked carefully, "Why should I look pretty, rather than efficient?"

He grinned. "Mike used to be a glutton for girls. With a spot more make-up and a less clinical-looking dress, you might remind him of the good things he'll miss if he doesn't get shuffling on that leg."

"You engaged a physiotherapist, Mr. Ryland! This may be Morocco, but we all happen to be English, and we'll behave that way, if you don't mind."

He gazed curiously at her bright cheeks and eyes, her parted lips. "You *are* young," he said, with tantalizing softness. "What made you apply for this job?"

"I had reasons." She cast a fleeting look over his face, apparently taking in the distinctive jut of his jaw and nose, the peak of dark hair in the centre of his forehead, the keen, sea-coloured eyes. Her glance lowered. "I have to work with the local doctor, of course."

"He's French," he told her gently, mockingly. "What were you running away from when you left England?"

Sally ignored this. "I'd still like to meet the doctor before I see your cousin. Will you arrange it?"

"Why not? I'll get him over early in the morning, and we'll go to Mike's house directly afterwards." He dropped the unlighted cigarette on to an ashtray. "May I ask your first name?"

"It's Sally."

He nodded. "Thanks for that concession, Sally Yorke. Shall we leave it that the doctor is our first appointment tomorrow morning?"

"Yes, I think so. I hope very much that I shall be able to help your cousin," she ended abruptly.

His dark brow lifted. Patently, he was unaccustomed to Sally's type of woman. But his tone was suave.

"You're a country girl, aren't you?"

"Yes, from Cumbria."

"What made you take the job at the Beckmoor Home? It's a bleak spot, isn't it?"

"It's lovely in the summer. I wanted to work with children, and the post was open."

"Didn't you feel you'd like to go a little wild after your training was finished?"

"No, I'm afraid I didn't; I'm just not that sort. In our family we all have an opportunity of training for something, and I chose physiotherapy. The Beckmoor, as you know, is in Yorkshire – near enough to my home for me to go there at the weekend quite often."

"Do you belong to a large family?"

"Fairish – a sister and three brothers. Except for one brother, we're all farming types."

"That explains your candour." He got up, a tall, wide-shouldered figure towering above her chair. Then he moved towards the door. "Make yourself at home in the suite, Miss Yorke, and if there's anything you need just ring for it."

She came to his side. "Thank you. I hope I'll have some success with your cousin."

"So do I," but he sounded doubtful.

He had half opened the door when someone knocked quickly and looked into the room. She saw a man in his early fifties, not very tall but handsome in a florid fashion. His black wavy hair was streaked with grey, his olive-skinned features were heavy and regular, and his dark eyes were bright and kind as he suddenly became aware of Sally.

"I am sorry," he said with a thick foreign accent. "I thought you would be alone, Dane."

"We were about to part," Dane said in his most tolerant tones. "Monsieur Pierre de Chalain . . . Miss Sally Yorke, from England."

"Ah, you come to help your poor Mike, no?" beamed the older man.

"I'll do my best," said Sally.

"Pierre is a family man," Dane explained with a trace of

satire. "He's also my partner in the Hotel Mirador."

"A small partner," Pierre explained, "but I am certainly the manager here – a much more patient manager than Dane could be! The hotel was mine, mademoiselle – an old dirty place which could scarcely pay for my wine bill. Then comes Dane Ryland, with big ideas and the courage to carry them out. And now you see the Mirador, which is famous and has everything of the best. He is a genius in business, this Dane."

"I thought he might be," said Sally, smiling at the man because he was so extremely pleasant and frank.

Pierre de Chalain looked at her rather longer than was really necessary, a thoughtfulness in his expression. Then, very charmingly, he took her hand and bowed over it.

"Mademoiselle, you are a guest of the hotel. Will you allow me the privilege of dining with you this evening?"

"Miss Yorke," put in Dane coolly, "has arrived only today. She'll want meals served in her room till she's accustomed to the place."

Sally moved out into the corridor, inclined her head to the two men and walked along to her suite. She found her key and unlocked the door, crossed a white carpet which was thick enough to hide in and covered the whole floor, and stood in the doorway to the balcony. Then she turned and surveyed the sitting-room. The chairs were purple, the curtains lavender, and the tables and cabinet were of rich dark wood, handsomely carved. The open doorway showed a vast bed; its covers, and even the quilted head, which was delicately shaped, were lavender. Sumptuous, lulling and yet vaguely exciting, the whole atmosphere had been planned for the rich tourist. The upper floors, Sally learned later, catered for people of more moderate means, but in their way they were as exotic as this.

At the moment, Sally was not impressed. Everyone knew that such palaces existed, and for her the Hotel Mirador was merely the place where she was to board while attending to Michael Ritchie.

Her patient sounded as if he might be rather a problem, but then nearly all adults who had been crippled were a little difficult to start with. Actually, she found herself rather eager to meet the young man; he challenged. In his way, of course, Dane Ryland was an even greater challenge, because it had been quite obvious a few minutes ago that he was disappointed in Miss Yorke.

Sally hadn't wondered, back in England, what her employer would be like. She had seen the advertisement, felt that strange, urgent leaping of the heart when she had looked up the letter from Lucette which was postmarked at Tangier, and almost blindly written her application. Dane Ryland had stated, in a cool-toned letter, that she must present herself in London for an interview with a doctor who had been apprised of the details of the case. Within a fortnight, Mr. Ryland had engaged her and arranged for a London agent to send her an air ticket and French money. She hadn't thought about him at all, personally; she had merely taken it for granted that, as he was an Englishman, he would be a conventional type. Which was silly, of course, because a man who left his own country to enter big business in a land like Morocco was very unlikely to be ordinary.

She turned back and looked out at the vivid green of the palms, the darker green of flowering trees. The man had asked disturbing questions, had known at once that she was country-bred, and had even seemed certain of himself in suggesting that she came from a large family. He had expected her to show excitement over Shiran, had put on quite an aloof, arrogant stare when that other man, Monsieur de Chalain, had asked if he might dine with her.

Dane Ryland, apparently, was something of an enigma. Well-bred and occasionally good-humoured, clever and possibly overwhelmingly proud of the fact that he had put himself at the head of the Hotel Mirador. He was as different as anyone could possibly be from the happy-go-lucky breed to which the Yorkes belonged. Which didn't matter in the least. Sally would a million times rather be a Yorke than anyone else in the world!

When, she wondered, would she be able to get in touch with

Lucette? A letter first, of course, and then they must meet, either here in Shiran or in Tangier. Though Tangier, she half remembered hearing, was a cosmopolitan city of vice and gaiety. Far better to insist on Shiran, though it was possible that Lucette would no more be able to travel south than to make the journey to England. What on earth could it be, this muddle that Lucette hinted at so volubly, yet would not explain?

Sally bathed and changed, chose a plain white sleeveless linen. She used a dab of powder, a rub of lipstick, then went into the sitting room, where she paused to decide what to do. It was dark now, the sky beyond the balcony a velvety black spangled with stars. It would be good to have a walk down in that garden or on the esplanade, and while walking she could decide where to have dinner.

She walked downstairs, stood on a terrace which ran the whole length of the front of the hotel; then she moved along it diagonally, so that she came to the ornamental parapet with its spaced urns of flowering plants. Here she paused, to take in the wide esplanade, the endless strip of grass on the other side of the road, the regimented palms which had flowering ginger bushes between them. At least, Sally thought it was ginger bush, though one couldn't be sure in the darkness about a plant one knew only from picture books. Beyond the bushes stretched the sea, a murmurous nothingness sprinkled with silver coins.

So this was Shiran. Vivid, brilliant, glittering even more at night than during the day. Surely one of the most attractive places in the world, yet Sally still felt no pull. I'm too earthy, she told herself contentedly; if I marry, I'll go rustic in England for the rest of my life.

At the end of the terrace she found a flight of steps to the garden, and she would have descended had not someone else been coming up them. She waited, and in a moment was face to face with Pierre de Chalain.

He bowed charmingly, exuding wisps of French toilet perfume. "Ah, good evening, Miss Yorke. Surely it is not necessary for you to explore alone?"

"I quite like being alone, monsieur."

"You English are very strange. I have known my partner for more than four years and still I say it – you are very strange. If it is a stroll you are in need of, permit me to accompany you through the gardens. I would feel happier."

"Can one come to harm so close to the hotel?"

"But no, of course not. It is merely that you are young and alone . . . and a woman." Again the wide, kindly smile. "I am of an age to be your uncle, mademoiselle. You may trust me."

"I shall be happy to trust you, monsieur."

"*Bon*. Then let us walk. The steps are shallow and there are six of them. I was about to go in and instruct someone to replace the electric bulbs in the torches here at the steps. They must have been removed this morning while repairs were taking place, and the maintenance man has omitted to finish his job. However, so long as they are replaced before the diners come for their evening promenade . . ."

He cupped her elbow until she reached the path, dropped his hand and walked at her side. He was still on the same subject.

"I was not here when the repairs were made, or I would have seen to it that the lights were in order. Mr. Ryland is very impatient of errors, you understand, and he takes it for granted that every workman is capable of finishing his task completely. I, who have managed this hotel ever since it was rebuilt under his direction, know that most of us are fallible. That applies also to myself."

"It makes you human, monsieur. I'm one of those people who have to learn by experience, too. It's a little hard sometimes, but when you do succeed you feel wonderful!"

"Indeed," he said appreciatively as he glanced at her bloomy skin, her smiling red mouth and piquant profile, "you must have succeeded very often! You have a serene look, Miss Yorke. You are unspoiled, and I should say that you are generous and considerate." He paused. "There is someone I would very much like you to meet. I felt it up there in Dane's room when I first met you, and that is why I asked if we could dine together, but as you are not yet dining in public we must defer this important occasion."

"Oh, but I think I will dine downstairs. I'm not used to eating alone. At the Beckmoor we – the staff – used to have our meals at a long table."

"You liked it there, at the Home?"

"I loved the children, but the Home itself is rather drab. I'm hoping they'll have me back – they've given me my holiday plus a leave of absence."

He was still looking at her in the darkness – weighing her up, she surmised. And wondered why. His next remark was un-illuminating; he seemed to have changed the topic.

"In any language, home is where the heart is, mademoiselle. My heart is here in Shiran. I have lived here most of my life. It will surprise you to learn that I married an English-woman."

"Really? And yet you still think the English are strange?"

"It was twenty-seven years ago, and she died only fourteen months after our marriage. She was unusual," he said with sad whimsicality, "but I loved her. Now I have only our son."

"Oh, yes. Mr. Ryland said you're a family man."

"Tony is twenty-six." He waved towards the formal gardens at the back of the hotel. "You will like to walk here in the daylight. There is a pool full of tropical fish, also some fine garden seats, a number of rare trees. And there is the lawn where our guests sunbathe and sit under umbrellas, drinking whisky and American soft drinks," he ended with a touch of wry humour. "Shall we now go to dinner? I will advise you what to eat."

The dining-room of the Hotel Mirador was on a par with everything else in the place – spacious, pillared, heavy white linen on the tables, which were set with immaculate glass and silver. And numerous dark-skinned waiters under the eye of a shrewd *maître d'hôtel*. Pierre de Chalain seated Sally at a table for three near the wall and ordered a light wine from the hovering steward. Then, from the menu, he chose Crême

16

Maroc, Sole Brunot and Steak Charpentier. Brunot and Charpentier, he informed her, were business men who had to be honoured whenever they brought a party to the hotel for dinner. If mademoiselle would look down the dining-room to the right, she would see two large tables decorated with orchids; they were prepared for this evening's party.

"Do you often give functions for celebrities?" she asked. "I arrived during a garden party held by someone called the Caid."

He nodded. "The Moors like to hold their festivities either in a vast empty room or in the garden." He spread his hands and smiled. "As you see, we could not be more prosperous. And it is all due to Mr. Ryland."

She gestured youthfully. "It's not so difficult to have material success when you give everything to it. Maybe he never thinks of anything else but making money."

"No," Pierre said gently. "Money does not mean a great deal to Dane. He likes success, to have the reins of several businesses in his hands and to be responsible for all the people involved. In the matter of the Mirador he set himself a goal, and achieved it. It was the same with the phosphate mine, and I am hoping it will be the same with a date plantation which I am half inclined to purchase." He smiled. "You will not be interested in such things. Tell me what you think of the Crême Maroc."

The soup was excellent, and she told him so. They went through the courses, Sally inquisitively attempting a small portion of each. When dessert was placed on the table, she said she would prefer to have coffee upstairs in her room.

"I'd like to take my time over it and read a book."

"So you read!"

"Well, naturally." Sally liked the man, but she couldn't quite make him out. He seemed anxious to keep her here, yet several times he had been approached by a waiter with a message. "If you're needed in your office, monsieur, I'm quite ready to leave."

"But there is no hurry." He glanced over his shoulder

towards the wide entrance to the dining-room, got out cigarettes. "You smoke, mademoiselle?"

"I do, but not now, thank you."

"Then, perhaps . . ."

He had again cast a hasty look towards the entrance, and this time his expression cleared and he half rose. A slender young man of infinite grace was coming towards them. He was black-haired, beautifully tanned and incredibly handsome in the Latin style, but his eyes were so light in colour that Sally instantly labelled them golden. He was smiling, showing good teeth, and looking as if he found most things highly amusing.

"So you come at last," said Monsieur de Chalain severely. Then, in the next breath, he melted. "You can explain later what has kept you. Mademoiselle," to Sally, "I present my son, Antoine. Tony, this young lady is Miss Sally Yorke; she comes to give treatment to Dane's cousin."

Tony de Chalain lifted a black eyebrow. "Well, well, a girl from England. I'm honoured to make your acquaintance, Miss Yorke."

"Sit down, Tony," said his father with a touch of irritation. "Drink a little wine, and then you must escort mademoiselle to her suite."

"Before I eat?"

"Certainly before you eat. We have dined already. You may dine later." Pierre had remained standing. He bowed to Sally. "I feel I can no longer leave my duties. Many thanks for your company at dinner, Miss Yorke. Goodnight."

She answered him, and as the man moved away she looked at his son, who was seating himself opposite her at the table. She felt laughter in her throat, for he was grinning and a wicked gleam danced in his eyes.

"The old chap's transparent, isn't he?" Tony said calmly. "He's never before hung on at the table for me. While I'm in Shiran I come and go here just as I please. Do you mind having me thrust at you?"

"Is that what's happening?" she asked vaguely. "I don't get it."

"Never mind – it's extremely pleasant. Are you sure you can't eat a second dinner?"

"Very sure. What exactly is your father trying to do?"

He gave her a smile which was as gentle as Pierre's but more knowledgeable. "You'll find out. I must say he knows how to pick 'em. You're quite a looker – in a frighteningly natural fashion. May I call you Sally?"

"If you like. Why does naturalness frighten you?"

He groaned. "Don't take me up on things I say, there's a sweet. I've a French father and dark looks, but I haven't the Frenchman's turn of phrase. I was educated in England."

"Where do you live now?"

"I've been staying forty miles away, at El Riza. My father drove down to see me a couple of days ago and we came here together late this afternoon. The poor old chap takes life heavily."

"That's no way to speak of your father!"

Her tone surprised him; he widened his eyes at her. "He said you were different, and you are. Oh, yes," as it was her turn to look astonishment, "he's already told me about you. Met you in Dane's office, apparently, and was instantly floored. Yet I shouldn't call you a dish for a Frenchman. It's that scrubbed, honest look about you that must have nailed him."

"You're a very odd person, Monsieur de Chalain!"

He laughed. "Just Tony. Tony, who never sticks to anything for more than a few weeks, who needs a wife who is steady and strong in spirit, but young and tender enough to rouse his protective instincts and be a good companion as well as a firm guide. Recognize yourself?"

Sally sat back, appalled. "Oh, really, you're going rather far. I'm quite certain your father thought nothing of the kind!"

"You don't know my father. You don't know me, either." Tony drank some wine, rested both hands in front of him on the table and leant towards her, confidingly. "It's only fair that you should understand the set-up. I've been living with a family in El Riza – the son is my friend. They have vineyards and olive groves, and for some time I've been helping out –

much to my father's disgust. He's been trying to persuade me to work here in Shiran, but I'm not interested in commerce. I haven't been here for some weeks, because each time I showed up it was a signal for the old man to press home the necessity for a career. Well, in the end he came to me – and several things emerged. I want a business of my own – a date plantation."

"He mentioned something about it," she said. "Mr. Ryland is to be consulted, isn't he?"

Tony nodded, sceptically. "But he won't touch it. Dane can pick up a lame proposition and make it tick in no time, but I can't see him doing it for me. After all," philosophically, "I've never given him reason to believe I'm worth it – so you couldn't blame him for turning me down, could you?"

"Have you already found a plantation?"

"Yes. It's gone wild and the dates have deteriorated, but there's no doubt that with cash it could be made into a first-class proposition. My father is willing to use most of his capital to purchase the property, but the administration and improvements would have to be covered by as much again. If Dane backed it and floated a company, the thing would succeed."

"Like this hotel?"

"That's right. You should have seen this place five years ago!"

"Yes, I've heard about it." Sally smiled and gave a small shrug. "Well, I hope you'll get your plantation, some way or other. I must go now."

"Not yet. You haven't told me anything about yourself!"

"There's nothing to tell. I'm not like you. I already have a career and I love my family. In fact, I'm far too normal to be interesting."

"But don't you realize that the normal is outlandish here in Shiran?" he said engagingly. "I'm beginning to wonder whether my father isn't rather a good judge of English-women."

"Now you're being silly. Your father is much too sensible to jump to conclusions about someone he doesn't know."

He reached over and took hold of her fingers, gripped when she made to withdraw. "It's all right – the French do this kind of thing, so it won't matter if we're seen. I'm only clutching at you to make sure you don't get up. Look here, Sally, you and I ought to get together. If you're staying for some time you'll be deuced lonely without an escort, and I'll promise to be no more than friendly. We'll find heaps to talk about."

"I'm here to do all I can for Michael Ritchie," she said flatly. "I want no complications of any kind."

"Mike," he said. "Yes, of course. Met him yet?"

"No. I'm going to see him tomorrow."

"Mike and I used to be buddies, but he's gone peculiar." He reverted to the earlier topic. "I don't want any complications either, but apart from Dane and Mike I'm probably the nearest thing to an Englishman you'll get in these parts. You'll expire from boredom if you don't have someone to show you round. Besides, I think we'll amuse each other, don't you?"

"We might," she admitted. "Let's wait and see, shall we? I must go now."

But Tony was slow in releasing her hand, too slow. Someone paused beside their table, looking down at them with cool, sea-green eyes.

"Good evening, Tony," Dane Ryland said. "No, don't get up. Order your dinner. I'll take Miss Yorke to her room."

But Tony stood swiftly, his smile faintly embarrassed. "Hallo, Dane," he said. "I tried to get in to see you, but you were busy."

"Make it ten o'clock tonight at my rooms. Ready, Miss Yorke?"

Without looking at him, Sally got to her feet. She nodded goodnight to Tony, and preceded Dane from the dining-room, her head held high. Small spots of colour had sprung in her cheeks and a vexed brightness shone in her eyes, but she went straight to the lift and did not demur when Dane followed her into the compartment. The door slid across, the attendant pressed a button and they ascended silkily to the first floor. Again she preceded Dane, walked along the corridor and

21

stopped at the door of Suite Seven.

She turned to him abruptly. "What do you propose to do – lock me in?"

His smile was bland. "Come now, Miss Yorke. You've had a long day. I thought it was understood that you'd dine in your sitting-room."

"You thought wrong; I didn't say I would. I'm accustomed to taking plenty of exercise, and even after a few hours I did need a change from the suite."

"You soon found a friend. Have you discovered that Pierre de Chalain has plans for Tony – plans which include the steadying influence of a wife?"

From him, too? It was unbelievable! Sally stared at him. "Tony de Chalain said as much, but I decided he was a little mad. I arrived in Shiran only this afternoon, intent only on my job and . . . well, that's all. Monsieur de Chalain and his son are strangers to me. How can you possibly have such wild ideas?"

"They're not so wild. Pierre would give an eye to see Tony settle down to business and take a sensible wife, but his trouble was to find the right type of girl. This afternoon," he observed with irony, "you stepped right into his path, and he feels you may be the answer."

"Did he tell you that?" she demanded, aghast.

"He didn't have to. I knew he'd gone to El Riza to see Tony and that he'd come back full of worry – he's done it before. If you remember," he added dryly, "I was there when you met Pierre, and when he told me that Tony had agreed to leave his friends at El Riza and come to Shiran until his future is settled, I knew the way his thoughts had flown. He's going to make an all-out bid to get Tony established."

"As far as I'm concerned, it's fantastic. I want no part in it!"

"Good for you, Sally," he said negligently. "It's best to be clear about things from the beginning. In any case, a girl like you couldn't settle in Morocco. You'd be pining all the time for cool green hills and woolly sheep."

22

Sally curbed the rising flames. "You don't have to be contemptuous of humdrum people like me, Mr. Ryland. We've a good many things that you haven't, and most of us prefer to stay the way we are. I'm not responsible for the ridiculous notions of your partner and I certainly don't want to know anything more about them. If you think . . ."

But his hand closed so tightly over her arm that she winced and stopped speaking. Three people were coming along the corridor, a bald and prosperous American, his enamelled wife and an incredibly svelte daughter. Dane bowed to them, charm in every line.

"Good evening, madame . . . monsieur . . . mademoiselle. I trust you will enjoy your dinner."

"We've never stayed in a finer hotel, Mr. Ryland," cooed the middle-aged siren as they passed. The blonde daughter slanted Dane a come-hither look but was silent.

When they were out of earshot, he looked down at Sally. "You were saying?"

"Nothing," she flashed at him in quiet fury. "You're just a machine, something that can be fed with any old thing and turn out a luxury article. And I believe I know the way you work!"

"Really?" he asked mildly. "Tell me."

"You suppress every human instinct. You grew up without loving anyone, and now the only sort of feeling you're capable of is . . . is the sort you have for your cousin. You'll pay for him to be whole, but you don't understand in the least what's really wrong with him – the anguish of a young, active and carefree man who is suddenly cut off from everything that means most to him. How could you understand? You've never loved *people*!"

"No?" he said laconically.

"No. If you could love, you'd be married by now."

"That's a startling theory; I must give some time to it."

"Don't bother. You just aren't the marrying kind."

"Now that's rather clever of you," he said admiringly. "I'm *not* the marrying kind. But don't let it get you; I'm pretty

23

normal in other respects." He paused. "I believe you're angry because I prised you loose from Tony de Chalain. Ah well, life is full of small disappointments. You'll get over this one. You know something? The more I see of women, the more thankful I am that I've never been tempted to probe below the surface of any of you. All women resent a bachelor."

"Chiefly because bachelors are often so selfish and conceited that they aren't a bit nice to know!"

"That sounds like a cue for an interesting discussion," he told her equably. "I may take you up on it some time." He took her key and opened the suite door, stood aside for her to enter. "Have an early night," he said. "You need a rest. The doctor will call in at about nine tomorrow morning, and we'll go up and see Mike soon afterwards. Don't forget about wearing something special."

"I'm here as a physiotherapist – nothing more!"

He looked at her, calculatingly. "Are you sure about that? Somehow I've gathered that you've something besides your job on your mind, though I can't think what it would be, in Morocco."

"Goodnight, Mr. Ryland," she said stiffly.

He shrugged as deeply as a Frenchman. "Goodnight, Miss Yorke," he answered carelessly. "Don't look out at the moon – it might bewitch you into forgetting Cumbria for a minute, and that wouldn't do, would it?"

The door closed noiselessly. Before the man could have taken a step, she slipped the bolt home with a snap he must have heard – and felt better for it. She took a few paces, so that she could see the night through the french window. Dane Ryland must have known there was no moon; Sally was fairly sure that he was also convinced that her first action would be just this – a peering into the darkness in search of a magic she would rather not find. The man was impossible!

Then she remembered his urbane charm when the American family had passed them in the corridor, and it occurred to her, suddenly, that the same charm with heart in it might be irresistible.

"Sweet grief," she said aloud to herself as she prepared for bed. "As if I care whether he has a heart or not! All I want is a chance to earn my salary, and a few illuminating hours with Lucette."

And promptly she steered her memory back to the letter from Lucette Millar, and to the years before, when Lucette had been a school friend and spent all her holidays with the Yorkes, because the Millar parents lived in Antibes or Lucca or Athens or Tangier, and were never in England when she needed them.

After the end of their schooldays, Sally had seen little of the gay, scintillating creature she had admired and loved, but there were letters – smudged, scented missives which sketched a continental life that Sally could hardly believe in. Then, five months ago, came the one from Tangier, a cry from the heart. It seemed that the Millars' funds were low and the parents were trying to marry their daughter off to someone rich and repulsive. Lucette couldn't escape because she had no money . . . "but oh, Sally darling, how I long to get away from them all! If you were here with me we could run away together, but a girl alone wouldn't stand a chance in this country. I don't seem to have anyone at all that I can turn to for help, and you're so very far away. But I won't marry the horrid old thing! Only what am I to do? Sally, couldn't you please get a holiday and come out here? I know it would be expensive, but I do have a bracelet I can give you. You could sell it when you get back to England. Please, Sally. *Please*."

Naturally, Sally had been distressed, but there had been nothing she could do. No holidays were due, and she was loath to leave her small charges at the Beckmoor Home. She had written to Lucette, pointed out that she was twenty-one and free to sell her bracelet and travel to England on the proceeds . . . but there had been no reply, none at all. And as the weeks passed Sally had become alarmed.

The older Yorkes had never cared much about Lucette, so Sally decided it would be better not to mention her dilemma at home. But more and more often she wondered if she couldn't

25

have done something for her friend. She wrote again, several times, and finally there was the note from Mrs. Millar. An extraordinary few lines which stated the impossible – that Lucette was naughty to have ignored Sally, but that was her way, and it would be better if Sally returned the treatment!

Lucette, as Sally knew, was effervescent and flighty, capable of heaps of gay lies and lacking in wisdom; but she would never, for any comprehensible reason, drop Sally Yorke completely from her mind. Sally was the only close friend she had ever made. Therefore the deduction was obvious. Sally's letters had been intercepted, and eventually, to ensure that none slipped by and into Lucette's hands, Mrs. Millar had decided to put an end to them. To Sally, the knowledge was quite unnerving.

She had found herself scanning travel advertisements, and watching for the magic mention of Tangier. Then her eye had caught the word Morocco in an advertisement in *The Times*, and she had discovered that Shiran was about two hundred miles south of Tangier. In a dreamlike state she had written to Dane Ryland . . . and here she was, a little excited, a little apprehensive, but determined not to be intimidated.

Tomorrow she would get someone to type Lucette's address on an Hotel Mirador envelope, and send off a letter in it. With luck, and the Shiran postmark, it would get past Mrs. Millar. After its despatch, Sally would have to work and wait.

She got into one of the huge beds, snapped off the light and lay listening to the monotonous fluting of insects and a distant, unearthly wailing noise, which probably came from a holy man at prayer. She thought of houris with sullen, mysterious eyes showing above a veil, of handsome Bedouins and tents in the desert. And inevitably she thought of Dane Ryland, who was tall and careless and commanding, and definitely not the marrying kind.

And then, because she was young and healthily spent, Sally went to sleep.

CHAPTER TWO

DAWN in Shiran was sudden. At one moment the sky was dark but tinged in the east with an arc of glowing pink; then a blend of milky blue and flamingo pink spread quickly across the heavens, followed by a clear and startling azure. The sun was up.

Sensational, Sally admitted, as she looked down from her balcony at the palms and ginger bushes rising from the long strip of emerald green lawn beyond the esplanade. Behind the greenness stretched the sea, calm and silvery and edged with white where it lapped the pale gold sand. A very inviting sea.

She showered and was served with a continental breakfast of crescent rolls, golden butter and coffee. After it, she took her time over dressing in a lavender linen dress, used a dusting of powder and rub of lipstick and felt sufficiently keyed up to face the languid, moneyed world of the Mirador.

Down in the vestibule she unwittingly drew glances. The short bronze curls framed a clear pink and white face, the blue eyes looked upon the brilliant world with calm innocence, and her red lips were slightly parted, as if she were drinking in the atmosphere and hadn't quite the capacity for so much glitter.

"Ah, good morning, mademoiselle!" Pierre de Chalain came from a door which was half hidden beyond the corner of the reception desk. "You slept well, I am sure. You make our morning look stale!"

"Thank you, monsieur." She took in his delight and reflected a little of it. "This morning, I like your city!"

"That is splendid. You have plans for the day?"

"Yes, I think so." She smiled at him, thinking how simple and kind he was. Strange to feel such things about a man of more than fifty, but Pierre de Chalain had, no doubt, always been an uncomplicated, easily hurt human being. It was difficult to believe, in the searching light of morning, that he had

27

entertained odd ideas which linked her with his son. "I'm supposed to be meeting the doctor with Mr. Ryland."

"Ah. Already you think of your business here!"

"I have to, monsieur. Do you have the English newspapers?"

"They arrive by plane this afternoon. I will send one of each to your room."

"Thank you very much. Do you know, I'm beginning to wish *you* were my employer here in Shiran."

"I wish it myself," he answered gallantly. "I can imagine nothing better than to have some relative of mine in need of your assistance; if I were Dane, I would keep you here indefinitely, on a large salary!"

She laughed, murmured something and walked out into the hot shade of the terrace, feeling rather surprised that she, Sally Yorke from the farm, had been able to deal so casually with the Frenchman. She walked along the terrace and round to the side of the hotel, where people in gay cottons and beach-wear were sitting at tables under umbrellas, while a few swam lazily in the magnificent tiled pool and others sunned themselves on bright foam-rubber loungers. Someone placed a chair for her and she looked up to thank him. Oddly, some of the happiness which was beginning to pulse in her veins seeped away.

"Good morning," Dane Ryland said, in those crisp, forthright tones she remembered. "Like a cool drink?"

"Thank you, but it's too soon after breakfast." She sat down, and felt him lower himself to another chair. "It's quite a playground you have here."

He shrugged. "People have to relax – even rich ones. I suppose you always spent your holidays at home?"

"Yes, but the farm is only about thirty miles from the sea."

"Cold sea, too much sand and a whipping breeze?"

She looked at him, surprised. "Do you know our coast?"

"I've travelled, little one," he said, his smile sardonic. "I may even have driven past your farm, some time or other." A pause. "What's so wonderful about that place where you grew up?"

28

"Well . . . it's a beautiful old farmhouse. The walls are two feet thick, the floors are dark and shining, the rooms are big, even if the ceilings are low, and the front door is carved oak and even older than the house itself. We have a herb garden and a river with stepping-stones, and if you walk up the ridge behind the house you can see the moor and a lake on one side, and a flourishing market town far away to the left. And there's a scent," she ended softly, "which you don't get anywhere else in the world."

"That's probably true of any place," he said laconically.

She agreed. "I did notice the smell of Shiran as we arrived. It was sweetish with a bitter, tobacco-like aroma in the background. I seem to have become acclimatized, because I can't smell it now. But this hotel is somehow unreal, like something in a glossy advertisement."

"Really?" he said, cool and mocking. "That must be because you've stayed at home all your young life."

She regarded him candidly. "You don't like criticism, do you? I mean, you like it even less than most people do."

"I can get along with a capable critic any time," he answered, "but I can't say that I take to having a girl with a childish stare throwing her opinions about. After all, your yardstick is a disintegrating farmhouse in Cumbria . . ."

She broke in swiftly, "Our house will be even more lovely than it is now when this gilded palace is out of date! This may be a home to you, but that's probably because you've never known a real home. And then, of course, you created the whole atmosphere of the hotel; it means something to you."

"It means nothing at all – I simply happen to be part owner. To me, the hotel is merely a business proposition."

"Then why do you live here?"

He gave her the experienced but slightly jaded smile. "My dear child, a man has to live somewhere, and if he's logical, he lives where he can do as he pleases, at any hour of the day. Here I have a suite, service and excellent cooking, and I'm absolutely free of all entanglements. What more could any man desire?"

To Sally, of course, he was incomprehensible. She said, a little carelessly, "It's as well for us women that all men don't think that way. Most of us have the normal instincts."

He nodded tolerantly. "Marriage, and all that. Picked anyone out yet?"

"Good heavens, no."

"But you mean to marry?"

She sat up straighter. "You make it sound like one of your business propositions. I suppose you've managed everything in your life that way, but I haven't. I let things happen."

"What does that mean – that you'll marry the first man who asks you?"

"Probably – because he wouldn't propose unless I'd encouraged him, and I wouldn't do that if I weren't in love with him."

He laughed, lazily. "You've a long way to grow up. To you, romance means a subtle magic between two people and the inevitable wedding bells. What comes after – a couple of youngsters, and slippers and a pipe for hubby?"

"Perhaps not quite in that order," she said, her smile bright and demure. "But it sounds awfully pleasant."

"And you sound horribly inexperienced," he said tersely. "I can imagine nothing more grim than being tied to a wife and children for the rest of my life. I'd sooner live in bachelor quarters at the phosphate mine!"

Not a whit put out by his forceful tones, Sally smiled cheerfully. "Well, few of us think alike, do we? For that matter, being married to you would hardly be a picnic, in any case." Inconsequentially, she queried, "Where is this phosphate mine that you rescued?"

"About seventy miles away." His smile was amused but narrow. "You think I'd make a rotten husband?"

"Well, you're pretty self-sufficient, aren't you? You seem to have grown up without any aptitude for love. Who runs your mine?"

"The mine doesn't belong to me – I'm merely a director of the company." He sounded impatient and a little sarcastic.

"What's your definition of an aptitude for love?"

She rested an elbow on her knee and her chin on her fingers, and gazed thoughtfully at the floating bodies in the swimming pool. "I've never really thought much about it, but it seems to me you have to keep a sort of freshness in your mind and a feeling of harmony with other people. That way, you're ready for bigger emotions when they turn up."

"You think I've forgotten how to be fresh?" he enquired.

Sally laughed. "I daresay you have your moments," she commented, "and I'm quite sure you could charm a woman into believing herself in love with you – if you wanted to, that is. How in the world did we get on to this topic?"

His mouth had a mocking slant. "It's a perennial between the sexes. With a woman, one could start out discussing fertilizers or nuclear physics and still end up by dissecting love and marriage."

"I expect you've gone over the ground a good many times?"

"Afraid so. We get all kinds here, but most of them are single-purposed; they're after something unusual in the way of a husband."

"Sounds horrid. I don't wonder you're warped."

Sally had spoken idly, but a moment later she knew she had managed to put her foot in it. There were people laughing and chattering in several languages; there were Moors serving wines and mint tea, a good-looking uniformed boy carrying a tray of cigarettes, the splashing of water in the pool, faint music from the lounge, where older people were taking mid-morning refreshment. In fact, there was everything one might expect of a sumptuous hotel on the hot coast of Morocco. Yet she felt an icy breath of wind about her and knew it had nothing to do with the elements.

"Sorry to upset one of your theories," he said, "but with me you don't quite pull off that atmosphere of harmony you mentioned. Like a cigarette?"

She declined, and was relieved to see that they were being joined by a greying Frenchman in a tropical beige lounge suit. Dane introduced him as Dr. Demaire, and the man bowed and seated himself, looked Sally over both professionally and otherwise, and said he was glad she had come.

"I have only a few minutes, I am afraid. You have some questions to ask me about the patient, mademoiselle?"

She looked at Dane, then at the other man. "Aren't I working under you, Doctor? To some extent I was primed by the doctor in England, but he told me I'd be working upon your instructions. That was what he understood."

"Yes, naturally. But I am not an orthopaedic man, mademoiselle. Michael Ritchie himself has his X-ray films and the file from the hospital, but I knew enough about the case to give Mr. Ryland the details to send to England. When it is convenient, you and I will go through his file together – if you can persuade Michael to part with it." He turned to Dane. "You are going to see your cousin this morning, with Miss Yorke?"

Dane nodded. "Why not come along with us?"

"I am unable to do that, my friend. Your cousin has asked me never to go there unless I am called. While he is in such a frame of mind I can do him no good." His smile at Sally was very French. "I think you do well to bring a pretty girl for Mike. In time she may succeed with him."

"You're not much help," Dane said. "I want you and Miss Yorke to work together and get Mike on his feet."

The doctor shrugged. "Tell your cousin, Dane. When he agrees to it, I will be happy to place myself at his disposal. In any case, for a day or two it would be best for Mike and the mademoiselle to get to know each other, without prejudice. If I were you, I would not tell him that Miss Yorke is a physiotherapist."

"Never?"

"If he walks, perhaps, but not otherwise. They are of an age to enjoy each other – let them do so. If the chemical reaction is right, your cousin will soon stir himself to take the cure!"

Dane was non-committal. "Thanks for your advice, anyway. Wine or coffee?"

Regretfully, Dr. Demaire had to decline both; he took his

departure. He had to drive out to one of the kasbahs for the day. Dane left his unlighted cheroot on an ashtray and remained standing.

"We'll go up and see Mike at once – but I can wait while you change into something more delicious, if you like."

Sally stood up and shook her head. "I prefer to look what I am."

"Maybe you're right," he said offhandedly.

They walked across the grounds, and guests in gay play-suits and swimming gear smiled at Dane and eyed his companion. His dark head inclined this way and that as he passed the groups, and, instinctively, Sally knew that he would be glad when this particular crowd had given way to another which did not know him. These people had regarded him as the manager during Pierre de Chalain's absence and he was forced to be friendly with them; but it was a friendliness which, she was sure, he did not feel.

He took her to a car, which stood in a bougainvillaea-covered shelter, and saw her seated, backed out on to the wide main drive and swung round towards the esplanade. He turned left along a narrow, cobbled street between sheer, windowless white walls, and impatiently followed a laden donkey till the road widened into an offshoot from the souks. Sally saw olive trees and date palms, the remains of crenellated walls, which had once surrounded a fort, a few houses set in gardens full of flowering bushes and fruit trees.

It was to one of these houses that Dane took Sally. The house was small and white, with an arched terrace in the front and much climbing greenery at the sides, and a thin dark boy was clipping a leaf here and there and standing back to admire the effect.

As the car pulled in below the porch, Dane said quickly and quietly, "You're just someone staying at the hotel. A holiday-maker."

"Do I look like a holiday-maker?" she retorted. "Besides, I'm not up to Mirador standards."

He glanced at her with cold appraisal. "Don't ever say a

thing like that again – don't even think it! You're way above most of the people we get here."

"Good lord," she said soberly, staring at him.

Sarcasm came back into his voice. "That's about enough softness for one morning. Come in and meet Mike. If he's in a good mood, you'll like him."

"And if he isn't?"

"Seeing that you're a little contrary by nature, it's possible you'll still like him, Miss Yorke." Then, more quietly, "Play along, there's a good girl."

Astonished, and with an odd quiver in her throat, Sally went with him up the three shallow steps into the dimness of a tiled porch. Dane opened the door and she stepped into a cool hall, which showed a charming sitting-room through an archway.

Dane went first, called, "Mike! Where are you?"

He came from another room into the sitting-room, a red-haired young man propelling himself in a wheel-chair. Sally watched him as he looked up at his cousin, saw a tight smile on thin features, which once had been healthily tanned. Then she met Mike Ritchie's eyes, and was aware that the next moment they had deliberately looked past her.

Dane shoved his hands into his pockets. "Sally, this is my cousin, Mike Ritchie," he said conversationally. "Thought you might like to meet a friend of mine, Mike. Miss Yorke has just come over from England."

"How do you do?" said the young man perfunctorily. "Sit down, won't you?"

Sally sat. She watched the young man's profile as he turned to Dane. It was good but not handsome, and there were lines in his face that should not have appeared for another fifteen years. His mouth seemed to be perpetually drawn in and his eyes, which had once been a soft hazel, were now an opaque brown and permanently narrowed. With pain? she wondered, and thought not. This cousin of Dane Ryland's was no more than twenty-six or seven, but his mind had twisted and his outlook become bitter because he had lost the use of a limb.

Sally had often tried to put herself in the patient's place, to feel lost and worried and bitter and without trust. She had never quite succeeded because she was so well aware of the orthopaedic miracles which were happening every day, but she had realized the hopelessness of a healthy young man who is suddenly and completely laid low. Mike Ritchie's case, she thought, was a fairly simple one, and, considering he had smashed himself up in a sports car, he did have quite a lot to be thankful for.

Dane was saying, "I'm sorry I didn't get along yesterday, Mike. The Caid gave a party, and Pierre didn't get back till late in the afternoon. By the way, Tony is with him."

"I don't want to see him."

"You don't have to." Dane leaned back in his chair. "He wants a date plantation in the El Riza district."

This drew no comment. Mike Ritchie sat there as conscious of Sally as she was of him, yet he looked only at Dane, or at the window beyond the broad shoulders. Obviously, this girl could go back to wherever she had sprung from.

"May we go into the garden?" she asked.

Mike hesitated, as if the request startled him. Then he said, "Dane will take you."

She stood up brightly "Can't we all go? Let me push the chair – I know the wheels dirty your hands when you're outdoors."

For the first time Mike looked at her, rather oddly. He shook his head abruptly. "Dane will take you! I'll have drinks ready for you when you come in."

"I much prefer to see a garden with the owner of it," she confessed.

"Well, Dane *is* the owner!"

"I'm sure he doesn't know much about gardens."

"You're wrong, young Sally," remarked Dane, with a lazy inflection. "I designed the grounds of the Hotel Mirador." He paused. "Perhaps we'd better have that drink now and get moving. I'll fetch some ice."

He went out, and Sally remained standing, only a foot or so from the wheel-chair and looking through the window, as Mike did. Dane had left her purposely, she knew, but she couldn't think of a thing to say to the young man – nothing that made sense, anyway. He was so tight within himself.

She prevaricated. "You remind me of someone I once knew. He wrote songs."

"What are you trying to say?" he asked tautly. "That I should forget my body and try to find some way of using my brain?"

"It helps, you know." Then, very suddenly, she said, "I can do quite a lot for you, Mr. Ritchie – physically, I mean. There's no reason why you shouldn't be driving a car again within a year."

He swung the chair, blazed up at her with those brown eyes. "So you're a nurse! Dane brought you here as a friend, because he hoped you'd make an impression on me. Well, you have, but the wrong kind of impression. Do me a favour, Miss Yorke. Go back to the Hotel Mirador and have fun with the playboys, and when you're fed up with it, go home! I don't want to see you again!"

Sally kept her balance. "Not very polite, are you? It's time someone taught you that having a game leg doesn't entitle you to be a boor and a burden. You're sick to death of yourself – I know that. I also know that you could get round on crutches . . ."

"I do, when it's necessary!"

"I'm glad to hear it, but it should be necessary more often. Exercise is vital – you don't need me to tell you that."

"No, I don't. I don't need you or anyone else to tell me anything!"

Dane sauntered into an atmosphere which was slightly electrical. He poured tall drinks and handed them, raised his own and smiled nonchalantly.

"Happy days," he said, and drank.

Five minutes later he was driving Sally back to the hotel. She sat beside him, perplexed but not defeated, and told him of the exchange between his cousin and herself.

Dane gestured. "You're in too much of a hurry. You ought

36

to have had half a dozen companionable talks with him before letting him guess you were brought here expressly for him. We'll go up again in a couple of days."

She shook her head decisively. "No. From now on, I'll manage him alone. It so happens that he can't kick me out or escape. I'll be like the Old Man of the Sea. He'll see that it's easier to give in a little than to shake me off."

"You'll find it wearing."

"Not if it does some good." She thought before asking, "What was he, before the accident?"

"A journalist. He reported on North African affairs for a couple of English papers."

"That's splendid. He could write something else – or even carry on with the reporting to some extent."

"Possibly. He dropped everything, though, and I doubt whether you could make him pick up the ends. Get him fit and he'll start living again." He smiled at her tolerantly. "You might have done better if you'd worn something continental."

"I'm not selling myself," she said shortly, "not even to a patient."

"In any case," he commented equably, "you might look odd in anything but clinical linen or English tweeds. All right, child, go ahead in your own way. Don't forget what I promised you."

"The trousseau? I won't."

He looked her way again. "Got someone in mind?"

"Not yet. Supposing I earn the trousseau before I find the husband?"

"It's a problem, isn't it? Not fair to make the offer without providing a man to go with it. Very well, I'll have a go at that angle, too. Any particular type you prefer?"

His mood and the topic excited her a little, but she sounded modest as she answered, "I like them solid, with a sense of humour and not too much imagination."

"Just what I'd expect. What about cash?"

"It's not important, but I would like him to be good with

his hands – you know, someone who's keen on making things."

"Such as cow-pens and kids' toys?" he asked with lifted brow.

Something in his voice put her quickly on the defensive. "Why not? They're both necessary."

"Oh, sure. I think I know the brand, but we don't get many of them in Shiran. Maybe after you've lived here a week or two you'll change your ideas." He slowed to enter the courtyard of the Mirador, said abruptly, "I've just decided something. We'll forget the trousseau and I'll give you a bonus cheque instead."

"Very well, Mr. Ryland," she answered, as distantly. "Thank you for the lift. I shall now be able to find my own way up to Mr. Ritchie's house each day."

"You'll do nothing of the sort," he said evenly, as he braked. "A car will be at your disposal. All you have to do is ring the desk when you want it."

"All right, if you insist."

"I do. The car will wait at the house each time to bring you back."

"I see." With her hand ready to open the door, she said, "About my room; I don't need a luxury suite. In fact, I'd be happier on the next floor in a bed-sitter."

"You'll keep Suite Seven," he said briefly. "That's an order."

He gave Sally no time to make an exasperated reply, but came round and opened the door. They entered the Mirador together; he led her to a seat in the lounge and called a waiter.

"Serve mademoiselle," he said. Then bowed to Sally as if she were a guest. "I've things to attend to. Excuse me."

He was gone, striding carelessly out into the vestibule to greet a couple of French business-men in white who sported huge cigars. Sally relaxed and ordered iced grenadilla.

It had not been a very rewarding morning, she thought. Mike Ritchie didn't want to be helped, and Dane Ryland was sceptical of her powers of persuasion. Sally wasn't too confident about them herself, but she meant to use them for all she was worth. She would have to be careful and dogged.

After which decision she felt calm and cheerful.

Just before dinner that evening, Sally decided to take a walk in the hotel grounds. Beyond the lighted terrace were the usual star-shot darkness, the black spikes of the palms, the scents released by coolness, and she ran down the steps to enjoy the breeze which rustled through the trees. But on the driveway she almost collapsed with fright as someone stepped from behind a sizeable bush and caught her arm.

"It's Tony," he said in conspiratorial tones. "I've been hoping you'd come out for the traditional breath of air. What about going somewhere else for dinner?"

"Like this?" she said blankly, indicating the striped glazed cotton she wore.

"You look heavenly to me," he said. "I know a place where we can relax. Game?"

"Well . . . yes."

"Good. We'll use the old man's car."

He took her hand and led her swiftly round to the side of the hotel. He put her into a biggish limousine, which had seen many years but only a few thousand miles. It moved well, even under Tony's impatient hands. He drove down the esplanade and turned along one of the innumerable narrow lanes of the town, which at this hour was crowded with Moors and Berbers in white and striped djellabahs, a few beggars and water-carriers, and vendors of the syrupy concoctions beloved by the population.

When they entered a wider thoroughfare which showed a white mosque against the skyline, Tony's graceful dark head turned towards her for a moment.

"Dane squelched my idea about the date plantation. My father's willing to whittle his bankroll to nothing to buy it, but Dane won't put up the capital to develop the thing. He's sure I have an ulterior motive."

"And have you?"

39

"That's hard," he said in hurt tones. "I want to settle down."

"Perhaps Mr. Ryland finds you a little too sudden. With a man like him you have to prove yourself before he'll believe in you."

"Have you found that out, too?"

"Yes, but I'm not worried." She paused. "You used to be friendly with Michael Ritchie, didn't you?"

He lost the little-boy lightness and nodded. "We had some good times together. He'd get an assignment and we'd both chase up to Algiers or Tunis and wade into whatever was going on. That was a peach of a car he smashed up."

"It was a good physical specimen he damaged, too."

There was a silence. Then Tony said, "It was worse for Mike than you or anyone else can know. There was a girl he wanted; the minute she knew he'd lost the use of his leg she dropped out."

"That was a terrible thing to do," she said soberly. "I knew there must be something more than just the paralysis of the leg when I saw him this morning. As if that weren't bad enough, he has to lose faith in himself as a man. Who was the girl?"

Tony shrugged. "Her people had a villa for a while and she drifted about the Mirador. I'm not sure that it would have lasted with Mike, but the crash came just as the affair was near the climax. I suppose the idiot came out of the ether convinced that he would never attract another girl in his life. He didn't help the doctors at all. All the rest of his injuries cleared up simply because he was one of those disgustingly healthy types, like Dane."

"Didn't Mr. Ryland guess anything about this girl?"

"Why should he? Mike always had a sweetie in tow, and this one was no more remarkable than the others." He waved a hand towards a stretch of coloured neon. "The bright lights of Shiran. You may have your choice between Le Perroquet and the Chapeau Vert. Both are semi-night-clubs with a distinctly French flavour, though they're completely harmless at this time of the evening. Le Perroquet is the prettier, isn't it?"

It was indeed, with its tubs of flowers in the entrance and the nodding parrot in neon tubing overhead. Tony led Sally into the vestibule, where they were taken in hand by a smiling steward. They were conducted into a dining-room, where gaudy murals depicted a human-looking bird in many postures, and given a table which was half screened by pot plants.

The dinner was not of Mirador standard, but it was adequate, and the floor-show which began at nine was astonishingly modest. Tony explained that the atmosphere did not "hot up" till midnight.

"And what happens then?" asked Sally ingenuously.

Tony grinned charmingly. "Another floor show, different wines," he said. "I first came to Le Perroquet on my sixteenth birthday. In some ways we were very French, you see. I was educated in England and spent all my holidays here. I used to take hair-raising tales back to school, and because my home was in Morocco they were believed. In fact, though, Shiran is no more evil than Brighton. It's just a lot more attractive!"

Sally was enjoying herself, but she had not forgotten the reason she was here in Shiran. That was why, a little later, she asked him casually, "Why aren't you friends any longer with Mike Ritchie?"

Obviously, Tony heartily disliked controversial topics. He looked uneasy, and smiled. "I went to see him in the hospital and he told me to clear out – said he never wanted to see me again."

"Seems to be a habit he has. He said the same to me this morning." She squashed out her cigarette. "We ought to go now, I think. May we drive a little way before we go back to the Mirador?"

Tony's expression was a comic blend of surprise and alacrity. "I never expected that sort of invitation from you, Sally. Of course we may!"

She said firmly, "I mean exactly what I said – a short drive and then back to the hotel."

"Oh, well, that's better than an early night. Let's move."

They left the dining-room, came into the vestibule once more, and were bowed on to a crowded pavement. There were French officers, an Arab in a white burnous, a few small boys, all of them interested in the long silver and blue car which had pulled up outside Le Perroquet. Sally watched, wide-eyed, felt little feathers along her skin as Dane came round from the driver's seat and helped his companion from the car. She was a pale honey-blonde with dark eyes and a form-fitting gown in silvery blue. About her shoulders she wore a blue mink cape, and the hand with which she held on to it glittered under the weight of a magnificent sapphire and several diamonds.

For a long moment Sally looked up into Dane's eyes. Then his cool, arrogant glance shifted quickly to Tony, and he nodded to the two of them. That was all. The jewelled hand slipped into the crook of his arm and they passed into Le Perroquet.

Feeling slightly stunned, Sally walked a few yards with Tony and took her seat in Monsieur de Chalain's car. They were drawing away from the lights when she asked, "Who was the creature in glorious Technicolor?"

"She's some baby, isn't she?" he said. "Her name is Cécile Vaugard and she sings love songs in a husky voice; I believe she also sings opera in a rather better voice. Every year, for a few weeks, she appears at Le Perroquet."

"A flame of Dane Ryland's?"

"You might call her that. He's always her escort while she's in Shiran."

"I thought he didn't care about women."

"He's almost human sometimes." Tony gave a laugh. "Cécile's got up like that for the public. Between times she puts on the homely act. She's half owner with Dane of the phosphate mine."

"She doesn't look like a business woman."

"Not phosphates, anyway," said Tony with an engaging leer. "Actually, she found herself owner of the mine when her father died, but it was losing so much money that she closed it down. Then she met Dane and told him about it; he took it on, put in new equipment and a couple of mine experts, and now it's so prosperous that Cécile sings only for fun and glory.''

Sally was quiet for some time. She looked out at the trees and the gimpses of the sea, saw in the distance the undulating walls of the medina. Then she realized that they were speeding into darkness.

She said suddenly, "I don't think I want a drive after all, Tony. This is only my second night here and I find myself a bit tired. Do you mind taking me back?"

"Of course I mind," he said ruefully. "Will you go out with me again?"

She promised she would, and said no more. At the Hotel Mirador she said goodnight to him almost abruptly and walked quickly to the lift. In her room, Sally did not pause and think. With an oddly stubborn smile on her lips, she sat down at the beautiful little writing table and began a letter home.

CHAPTER THREE

SALLY had always lived very much in the present, and when she awoke next morning it was with the usual sensation of this being another day for her to use as best she could. But when she had slipped out of bed and on to the balcony, she remembered last night and her own extraordinary feelings. For there below, dropping a bathrobe and taking a header into the swimming pool, was the muscular figure of Dane Ryland. No idling for him by the poolside, no delicious floating with the sun warming his body. A dive, several lengths of powerful over-arm stuff and then a leap up on to the marble. His morning swim was as much of a business, apparently, as the hotel or his other interests.

Determinedly, Sally backed into the bedroom and hummed to herself while she took a shower and dressed. She ate the usual light breakfast which was brought to the suite, and went down to the esplanade for a walk. She found some colonnaded shopping streets, covered souks which were crammed with men in robes and women who were only distinguishable from the men by their yashmaks. A little shy of buying from people who did not understand English, she returned to the Mirador and entered its emporium, a splendid store whose plate-glass windows walled a tiled corridor on the ground floor. She bought several sports shirts in gay colours, a sun-frock, harlequin sun-glasses, plaited straw slippers and a floppy straw hat.

The assistant promised to send the goods to her suite. "Number Seven?" he said with a bow. "I will charge them, mademoiselle."

"I don't have an account with the hotel," she told him. "I'd better pay you now."

The dark eyes looked comprehending. "You are the young lady from England? I have orders from Mr. Ryland that you are to buy what you wish, at no cost."

"But that's impossible. I could send you bankrupt."

He smiled, lifted his shoulders. "I doubt that, mademoiselle. Mr. Ryland was emphatic."

For a moment Sally was tempted to tell him to return the things she had chosen to their shelves and hangers, and then she grew vexed again. Bother Dane Ryland!

"Just give me a note of what I've selected and their prices," she said. "I'll deal with it later."

When her purchases were delivered to her room, Sally put the goods away, took a long glance at her neat blue reflection in the mirror and picked up the lavender-coloured telephone. "Reception? This is Miss Yorke. Will you arrange for me to have the car, please? Thank you."

Ten minutes later, hatless and carrying nothing at all, she got into the car and gave instructions. They were moving round the drive when she noticed the silver and blue creation parked in the middle of a line of more ordinary vehicles. She leaned forward and spoke to the driver.

"Does the big car belong to Mademoiselle Vaugard?"

"But no," he answered politely. "It is the private car of Monsieur Ryland."

"And this one, that you're driving?"

"It is also monsieur's."

Sally sat back. One for weekdays and one for best, it seemed.

Determinedly, she took a lively interest in the tortuous streets and the hillside, which lay glittering under the sun. She saw a shrine that she hadn't noticed yesterday, and a beautiful Moorish house, which must belong to some notability, possibly the Caid. Even speeding past it in a car, she could see pillars of bright mosaic tiles, and an expanse of sculptured stone above an elegant doorway. One day, perhaps, she would have an opportunity of looking over such a house. She hoped so.

But as they turned on to the small drive outside Mike Ritchie's house, Sally brought all her mind to bear on the present. She told the driver to park in the shade and wait, walked lightly up into the little terrace and reached in to nock at the open door. Then she took a step into the small hall and stood there in its coolness, waiting for something to happen.

The thin youth who had yesterday been clipping the shrubs came into view from a corridor. He bowed, said nothing and walked away, to return within a minute.

"Monsieur is sorry, but he cannot see you, mademoiselle. Please be seated and I will bring some tea."

Sally shook her head. "No tea, thank you. Tell Mr. Ritchie I'll wait till he's free."

The servant looked uncertain, but disappeared. Again he materialized, bearing a tray which held the glass of mint tea which is indispensable even to the poorest hospitality in Morocco. Sally accepted it and placed the glass on a dark carved table. She sat in a chair which was uncomfortably but cleverly thonged in many-coloured leather, crossed her ankles and relaxed as if she had all the time in the world.

Ten minutes ticked by, fifteen, twenty. Twice the servant's head appeared round the corner of the corridor, and twice he stared at her perplexedly and withdrew. Then, finally, came the sound for which Sally's ear had been waiting; a faint rumble and squeak on the tiled floor. The invalid chair rolled into view and Mike Ritchie, a red lock drooping over his brow, came to a halt about a yard from Sally's chair, and glared at her.

"What do you want?" he demanded.

She smiled, as if totally unaware of his anger. "Oh, good morning, Mr. Ritchie. I'm so glad you could see me. I'm alone today, and thought we might have a talk."

"I don't want your pity."

"Good heavens," she said with a show of surprise. "I don't pity you. You pity yourself so much that there's no need for anyone else to waste any on you. I came to correct a little misunderstanding. I'm not a nurse."

"No? Then what are you!"

"A physiotherapist. You must have met one before, at the hospital."

46

"There was a muscular creature of about fifty – no one like you." He lifted his head and gazed through the doorway at the hot greens and reds of the garden. "All right. Say what you came to say."

"Right here in the hall?" He didn't answer, so she went on casually, "Well, it was like this. Mr. Ryland was very worried about you because you wouldn't go back to hospital for further treatment. He consulted the specialist who set your various bones, and was told you needed physiotherapy; but there was no one here in Morocco who could help you. So Mr. Ryland advertised in England, and eventually engaged me. I may not look it, but I've had quite a lot of experience."

"Not with my sort of trouble."

"You mean the mental part – no, perhaps not."

He looked at her fleetingly. "What do you mean – mental part?"

She gave him her most disarming smile. "You see, I deal mostly with children, and they don't have mental troubles over their condition. They've had polio, accidents, diseases of the bone and nerves, but in the hands of someone wearing a white overall they're thoroughly contented and relaxed. It's so much easier to help someone who believes in everything."

"I'm not a child."

"Yet you're behaving like a certain type of child – the pampered type. We got a few of them at the Orthopaedic Home, but they'd mostly been tamed in hospital before we dealt with them. You're older, and therefore more stubborn."

"Is that all?"

"Well, no, it's only the beginning, but I didn't come to deliver a lecture, only to point out that with patience you'll probably be able to walk with one stick in less than six months. It seems so silly to refuse even to try it out."

"I know that whatever I go through I'll always be a cripple."

"At least you have your own leg, not an artificial one." She paused, her glance on his prematurely lined face. "You wouldn't want to be an emotional cripple as well, would you?"

47

There was a brief silence. Mike had tensed suddenly, as if startled and wary, but after a moment he spoke a little unevenly.

"I sensed yesterday that you see a little farther than most girls, and that's why I wanted you to stay away. Just leave me alone with it!"

She answered in reasoning tones, "I can't really. Mr. Ryland brought me here by air and he's given me a magnificent suite in the hotel. It's a costly business for him, and the least I can do is peg away at you till you give me a chance of doing all I can for you." Ostentatiously, she opened the cigarette-box and showed him it was empty. "May I have one?"

He took a box of fifty from his pocket, automatically flipped it open. She waited while he thumbed his lighter, leaned forward just a little so that he could light her cigarette, and stayed there, smiling at him. Mike drew back and lit his own cigarette, and she saw the fingers of his left hand curl rather tightly over the curved wooden arm of the wheel-chair.

"What has Dane told you about me?" he asked off-handedly.

"That you're twenty-six, a journalist, were keen on fast cars and attractive girls. I think he was rather disappointed that I'm not prettier."

"You might have been forty and tough."

"Oh, no, he took care of that. His advertisement insisted on a photograph. I happened to be the least ugly."

Mike ignored the unintended cue. "It's my fault you're here. If you want to leave, I'll offer Dane what it cost him to bring you."

Sally was vexed, but determined not to show it. "I don't want to leave; I simply want to do the job I'm engaged for. Tell me, do you always stay indoors?"

"Pretty well."

"How do you spend the time?"

"Reading and playing chess with an old chap who lives down the road."

"I play chess too, but not very well." She tapped ash into a tiny bowl, and then held the bowl near him so that he could

48

do the same. "This is a lovely little house. I suppose the Frenchwoman who made the garden furnished the place as well?"

"I believe so. Dane bought it more or less as it stands."

"For you?"

"For himself, probably."

"But he told me he wants nothing better than to live at the Mirador without domestic ties."

He shrugged. "Have you met Cécile Vaugard?"

Sally's breath caught for a second in her throat. "No, but I've seen her. She's ravishing."

"She's also a magnetic singer – and pure French. She's the only woman Dane ever bothers with, so one day – seeing that he always tries everything once – he'll take a wife, probably Cécile. When she's in Shiran, they'll live in this house, and for the rest of the year Dane will let a friend live here and go back to his suite at the Mirador."

"It doesn't sound much like marriage."

"But it will be as much as Dane will want." He gave a swift, irritable tug at the wheels of the chair and slipped back a yard or so. "Is there anything else you want to know?"

"Am I too inquisitive? I was quite enjoying the gossip." She squashed out her cigarette, dusted grains of ash from her skirt. "Don't you get lonely?"

"No." The thin line of his jaw tightened, emphasizing a chin which was narrow and a little obstinate. "In the course of several months one can evolve a new way of living."

"I suppose so, if it's necessary. But with you it isn't. You're just a mule, and unfortunately you're hurting yourself most."

"You don't say it the way Dane does, but then you're a girl and you haven't his colourful vocabulary."

"It doesn't matter how it's said, if it's true." She paused, and added clearly, "I'd like to come and see you with the doctor. Is that all right?"

"No."

"Will you allow me to give you some ordinary hand massage?"

"What's the good? I've tried it myself and it doesn't do a thing."

Sally sat very still. This was the first indication that he really wanted to help himself and she knew, intuitively, that he had never mentioned it to anyone else. One had to be casual with him, casual to the point of uncaringness.

"I'll send you some massage oil and you can try again. And, if you like, I'll show you some exercises to keep the rest of you in trim."

He sounded quite nasty as he said, "Trying to earn your keep?"

She stood up. "Don't blame me, do you? As a matter of fact, you aren't the only reason I came to Morocco. I'm trying to get in touch with an old friend of mine, and when I do, I shall probably fade out of Shiran. I only wish I knew more about the country."

Mike said morosely, "I've been around. What part of it interests you?"

"Tangier."

"It's a sprawling, complex city. Have you got your friend's address?"

She nodded. "I'll tell you about it some time – if you'll let me come again, that is. If not, I'll battle through on my own."

His glance flickered over her. He reached out and stubbed his cigarette in the bowl. "Are you thinking of going to Tangier?"

"Not yet. If I do decide to go, I'll find out more about it. May I come again, Mr. Ritchie?"

"It's a waste of time, but please yourself," he said ungraciously.

"Very well, I will. Tomorrow at ten." She moved towards the door, and then turned. "I read an article of yours last night, and found myself smiling more than once. For a man with a sense of humour you're horribly grim in the flesh, Mr. Ritchie . . . or may I call you Mike?"

"Call me what you like," he muttered, and closed his eyes.

Sally looked down at him with compassion, but knew better

than to touch him or the chair. He had lived with his defeat for so long that even the smallest battle was exhausting. Still, he had to fight, and she knew that the first onslaughts were the worst; once past them he would smile again and gather courage.

"Goodbye," she said softly, and went out into the blinding sunshine.

As the driver set the car moving away from the house, Sally tried to gauge whether she had accomplished anything. Very little, she decided, but Mike was stirred and that went to the credit side. He gave so little away that it was difficult to pinpoint the things which would really get under his skin.

Yet she was sure that before his accident Mike had been a normally high-spirited and gregarious young man, inventive, lively and full of fun. It was going to be quite a task, though, to convince him that he could be his normal self again. The loss of the power to walk and drive had stripped him of self-confidence, and the girl in whom he had been interested at the time had let him down so badly that he imagined himself as being unattractive to women for the rest of his life; it hadn't been that particular girl who mattered – only the fact that she had abandoned him in his most sensitive moment. And there was his job. He was the type to have loved the dashing about in North Africa, the interviewing spiced with danger.

Sally vowed to do all she could for Mike. Physiotherapy, she thought, would be the least of it!

The evening swim in the huge and magnificent pool was an excellent idea, Sally decided, as she took off her white bathrobe and pulled a cap over the bronze curls. The grounds were cool and scented, a faint breeze ruffled the water, and the only figures in sight were those of the servants moving between the balconies and the lower regions. She dived in and found the water warm and caressing, and far more buoyant than she had imagined. It was piped sea-water. She swam and floated, looked at the jewelled sky and told it she hadn't a trouble in the world.

She lay on her back, moving her arms lazily in cartwheel circles and watching the droplets slide from her fingers in the darkness. Then, distinctly, she felt a tickling sensation at the sole of her foot, and she pulled up her knees and sank them, to come face to face with Dane. Dane, who looked like a wet, mocking mask carved from mahogany.

"Hallo," she said. "I thought you swam in the mornings."

"I do, but I came out on to my balcony ten minutes ago and saw something interesting in the pool. It turned out to be you."

"Who did you think it was?"

"You."

She laughed. "Such flattery, Mr. Ryland! You came down to save bothering with a shower."

"Maybe. Come on out. I want to talk to you."

"Right now?"

"It's possibly the only place and time we can't be interrupted – everyone's too busy making themselves handsome for dinner. Come to the side. I'll pull you up."

But Sally swam farther, to where her robe had been dropped, and by the time she reached the spot Dane was crouching on the side of the pool and extending a hand. She took the leap and landed beside him, felt him sling the robe about her shoulders before he slipped down and sat as she did, with feet dangling in the water.

"I didn't bring any cigarettes. Do you mind?"

"No. Talk away."

"Give me time, little one. Even I prefer a few preliminaries occasionally. Is this your first dip in the pool?"

She nodded and pulled off her cap, shook back her hair. "It's delicious, isn't it? But I'm hoping to bathe in the sea some time. Your hotel guests don't seem to bother much with the beach."

"The Moors don't care for scantily-clad women, so we discourage communal bathing, except in our own grounds. But there are some lovely wild beaches along the coast where people picnic and swim in families. I'll take you some time."

"Why, thanks! I'll hope to deserve it."

He gave her a sidelong, calculating glance. "What does that mean – that you were unsuccessful with Mike this morning? You didn't report, so I took it you'd drawn another blank.''

Sally took the scuff of the terry-cloth robe between her fingers and rubbed an itch from her chin. "I don't think I did, actually. Mike told me a few things and he didn't tell me not to come again. He's terribly touchy, of course, but so heartily sick of himself that I believe he'll talk again. Why don't you go up and see him more often?''

"I go almost every day,'' he said briefly.

"But you don't stay long. Were you and he good friends before his accident?''

"Of course, but I'm eight years older than he is, and you'd be surprised what that means between cousins. Mike just galloped through life without a care. When he made errors he laughed, and very often made them again. He was always convinced that he led a charmed life – till he found he didn't. When he was younger I cured him of borrowing, but it took the smash to cure him of a craving for speed and admiration. He caved in.''

Sally said nothing for a minute. She dipped her toes lower and watched them, and at last said thoughtfully, "Under the dash and bravado he was sensitive, but no one ever found it out.''

"Mike's not sensitive – never has been. Don't kid yourself that because he writes he's one of these tender, artistic souls. With him, writing was mere reporting with his own individual twist.''

She said stubbornly, "It's the sensitive people who feel an incapacity like his so terribly. The reason he won't make the effort to regain the use of his leg is that he knows it will never be absolutely right, and therefore life will never be the light and airy thing it once was. There's no other kind he wants, so he doesn't try.''

Dane snapped his fingers sharply. "For heaven's sake don't talk to Mike like that. He's quite sorry enough for himself!''

"Of course I wouldn't,'' she said crossly. "Have I got to be careful what I say to you, too? I'm simply trying to analyse what's wrong with him."

"Well, leave it alone and stick to muscles!"

"You said you wanted me to persuade him to have treatment in a hospital."

"Do that, but don't start dripping emotion all over him, or he'll respond in a way you may not bargain for! You don't have to restore his faith in women. He'll do that for himself when he's fit to resume the chase."

"You bully, you," she said quietly.

Dane was silent for a surprised second; then he laughed. "You're an odd girl. I've always thought women were easy to understand, but you've a quirk in the usual feminine character. Maybe it comes of reaching the age of twenty-one without having wallowed in the usual calf-love affair."

"Who said I'd never had an affair? When I was training I was terribly gone on one of our lecturers."

"Really?" His tone scoffed. "Did he respond?"

"Vaguely. We tramped the moors a few times and he took me to an art show in York."

"Then what happened?"

"It fizzled out." She got back quickly to the subject of Mike Ritchie. "Your cousin swims, I suppose?"

"He used to. We'd often do a mile along the coast at weekends."

"It would do him the world of good to swim again, but he can't start in the sea and there are too many people about here at the pool. He wouldn't come."

He thought for a minute. "There's a lagoon along the coast, but before you can get Mike to enter it you'll have to persuade him to take the drive. Give it a couple of days and we'll talk again."

Sally knew that she should now get up and take her smiling departure, but something held her here, at Dane's side. She did get as far as slipping her arms into the robe, but the reluctance to move was so extreme that she felt pleasantly heavy and drugged.

Dane shifted, and when he spoke she noticed that his voice

had changed. "Do you prefer the food at Le Perroquet to ours at the Mirador?"

Sally had to adjust her thoughts before she could answer, "Oh, you mean last night. It was a change, that's all."

"Tony's idea, of course."

"Yes."

"He probably told you that I heartlessly turned down his plea for a date plantation."

"I understood his father was willing to buy, but you weren't interested in forming a company to make it a success."

"That's it, exactly." He had withdrawn. "In your leisure time here you're quite free, but I'm afraid I'll have to insist on your staying away from such places as Le Perroquet."

"You were there later than I was."

"I escorted Mademoiselle Vaugard. She has a contract to sing there at eleven each night, for two months." A pause. "I also happen to be a man."

"I didn't see anything wrong with the place."

"I doubt if you'd see anything wrong anywhere," he said coolly. "You're not in a village in England, you know. Morroccan women hardly ever go out, let alone enter restaurants and night-clubs, and the few French wives of the officials are strict in their ideas and behaviour. You're a resident here for the present – not a tourist who can hit the high spots and pass on."

"Very well, I won't go again."

"Good. And if I were you I wouldn't see too much of Tony, either. He's entirely without a sense of responsibility."

She said stiffly, "He's not an unpleasant companion and he does happen to be half English."

"He also has a father who'd go to some lengths to get him settled with a wife and a good living. I like Pierre and I can understand his ambitions for Tony, but I brought you here for a far different purpose."

"You needn't think I'll lose sight of that, Mr. Ryland!"

Dane remained cool and unperturbed. "I'm more concerned about Mike than you think, and I want results from your association with him."

Sally's usually even temper slipped slightly out of control. "What are you trying to say, Mr. Ryland? That I'm thinking of my own enjoyment before Mike's needs? When I'm not with him am I supposed to sit twiddling my thumbs? Are you afraid I won't earn my salary? . . ."

"Don't raise your voice to me, child," he broke in sharply. "If you're angry because I won't encourage your friendship with Tony de Chalain, it's too bad, and it doesn't make any difference. Seeing that you're impervious to the magic of Shiran, you shouldn't find it too difficult to resist Tony. I want no entanglements – do you understand?"

She jumped up, but, even so, he seemed to be standing before she was. "I think you're being beastly! If it weren't for Mike, I'd tell you to keep your horrid job and all that goes with it. You're detestable!"

His eyes narrowed, and glittered in the darkness. "Because I'm spoiling your first romance? That's a typically girlish reaction."

"Well, perhaps I'm typically girlish! I certainly couldn't be as hard and one-track as you are. I don't believe you ever think really deeply about anything except your soulless business propositions, and where Mike's concerned, he's just another proposition that has to be put back on to a sound basis. You generously spare him ten minutes a day, and order up someone who might be able to help get him shipshape. You don't really *care*, because it isn't in you to care about anyone . . ."

"That's enough!"

But Sally was breathless and defiant. Without shoes she was tiny beside him, but she flung up at him a reckless spate of words. "You can't frighten me, you big brute! I'm on Mike's side, and Tony's, and I won't be cowed. You sit back like some overlord and tell Tony he couldn't run a plantation if he tried. At times you get nasty with Mike because he won't make any effort for his own good. But if you cared to spare the time and a little feeling, you could help both of them tremendously. I don't wonder you've never married, and never expect to.

A man has to own a heart before he even thinks about such things!"

He gripped her shoulders and was probably in a mood to shake her violently. But suddenly the pool was flooded with light from overhead lamps, and Maynier, the secretary, was hurrying across the grass. With an audible breath, Dane released her.

The secretary stuttered. "Monsieur, I have been looking for you. Mademoiselle Vaugard is in distress. Her voice has gone and she demands you and Dr. Demaire."

"Her voice?" Dane sounded a little strange; the same note in any other man's speech might have denoted a swift gathering of wits. "Is she in pain?"

"She is much disturbed, monsieur."

"I'll shove on a robe and go along to her suite."

Maynier bowed. "Mademoiselle is already in your sitting-room, monsieur. She is lying on the couch."

Dane shrugged. "All right, Maynier. I'm going up."

He slipped a hand under Sally's elbow and gripped, marched her across the lawn to the side entrance which led to the private staircase. They went up together and at the door to Sally's suite they stopped, and he pushed open the door. Then, without a word, he walked on to his own suite.

Sally got out of her swim-suit and into some underwear and a plain dress. She ordered a salad and some coffee, ate and drank absently and was cross with herself for feeling despondent. The tray was taken, and she put out the light and sat in the balcony.

She thought back over the conversation with Dane, its light and rather exciting beginning, the swift deterioration into a one-sided slanging match. It had been wrong to speak to him like that, but she had stuck to the truth. He was too cold-blooded to care about people. Mike had to be helped because he was a cousin; every facility offered, no expense spared. Dane was generous in every way but the one that mattered most; he was too clever and aloof to give of himself.

Why Sally should resent his self-sufficiency she did not

know. It was ridiculous to care whether he had a heart or not, and futile to wish him different. She had a job to do here in Morocco, and she told herself that the sooner she completed it, the happier she would be. Upon which decision, she once more descended the private staircase to the grounds, and took a long walk. Such a long walk, in fact, that when she returned to the hotel it was nearly midnight, and many people were going upstairs to bed.

Sally came to the door she seldom remembered to lock, opened it and found that there were lights in the entrance hall and sitting-room. Her heart fluttering queerly, she stood in the doorway between the two rooms and stared at the woman who sat enjoying a cigarette in one of the purple chairs.

The woman spoke first. "I have not dismayed you, I hope. You are Miss Yorke, I believe? I am Cécile Vaugard."

Rather jerkily, Sally made some acknowledgment. She came farther into the room, felt herself tightening up as she waited for the other to say more.

Afterwards, she remembered thinking in that moment that this was not her lucky day.

CHAPTER FOUR

CÉCILE VAUGARD smiled, a bewitching smile which showed beautiful white teeth between her curving red lips. Seated, she looked smaller, and with the wheat-blonde hair smoothed back in deep waves and secured by a jewelled comb, her rich dark lashes enhanced by mascara and her creamy neck encircled by a single row of pearls and diamonds, she was spectacularly lovely.

"I thought it was time we should meet," she said in velvet tones. "You speak French?"

"A little – it's not so good as your English."

"But you have been able to make yourself understood in the souks?"

"Oh, yes. The Moors seem to be exceptionally intelligent."

"They are also excellent business-men. For money, they will understand any language." Cécile paused. "I would like us to understand each other, Miss Yorke, because I may be able to put you in touch with some work which will pay you more money than you have ever seen in your lifetime."

"Really?" said Sally, with caution. "I think you must have over-estimated my abilities."

"You are a masseuse, are you not?"

"Partly."

"You have dealt with children?"

"More than with adults – yes."

"Good. There is a Caid at the Kasbah of Nezem who has a small son in need of this therapy of yours. The child was a polio victim two years ago and he is left with some sort of trouble. He happens to be the Caid's favourite son, but neither the Caid nor the mother will allow the child to take treatment in a clinic. They have had Moorish and French masseurs, but no one from England. How would you like to become a member of the Caid's staff for perhaps six months? He would pay whatever you ask."

"I'm afraid it's impossible. I could no more guarantee to be successful than the others who have treated the child, and in any case, I'm already employed."

"By Mr. Ryland – I know that."

There was a brief silence, then Sally said politely, "You seem to have regained your voice, Mademoiselle Vaugard. Were you able to sing this evening?"

Cécile shrugged gracefully. "It has happened before, but Dr. Demaire has the remedy. Yes, I sang, Dane told me afterwards that he has never heard me in better voice."

Which was strange, thought Sally; the fleeting laryngitis sounded as if it might have been bogus. Still polite, she said, "I would like to hear you sing some time."

"When I arrived in Shiran I gave a concert at the Mirador. I shall do so once again before I leave – light opera, French ballades. At Le Perroquet they like the popular nostalgic songs, but I get tired of them." Cécile sank further into her chair. "It was you I saw in the pool with Dane this evening, was it not?"

Faintly startled and still wary, Sally answered, "Yes, it was. My first dip since I've been here, as a matter of fact."

"It was an arrangement between you – that meeting?"

"No, it was more or less accidental."

"Yet you seemed to be very close and interested in each other as you sat on the side of the pool."

"Did we?" Sally recalled those few minutes and thought how deceptive appearances could be. "We were talking about other people." Then she saw the hard glint in the other woman's eyes, remembered something, and stiffened. "If you manufactured the lost voice to break it up, you needn't have bothered, mademoiselle."

"How dare you!" But Cécile's tones remained smooth and without heat. "Yet I can see how you dare. Dane is English, so is this cousin of his whom you are to help. One cannot blame you for the ideas which naturally come to a woman's mind in such circumstances. After all, you come from a dull country farm. You are hoping to find a husband, no?"

Why not be truthful? "I hope to marry some time," Sally said, "but not in Morocco. As you remarked, the choice of Englishmen here is limited to Mr. Ryland, who couldn't care less about women – and Mike Ritchie, who has a chip the size of an oak tree on his shoulder. I'm here purely on business."

"That is something I cannot believe," stated Cécile. "Always inside a woman there is hope of romance. Even the English are not immune, or your population would have declined long ago. I am a Frenchwoman, Miss Yorke – therefore I am shrewd and a realist. Some day, perhaps, I shall marry Dane Ryland."

"Yes . . . I thought you might."

"So, naturally, I do not wish there to be small complications which might become big complications once I have left Shiran. You understand?"

"Perfectly. But I assure you I'm no threat to your plans."

"While I myself am here, no. But Dane is fond of his cousin Mike. If you were to awaken that young man's interest in life, Dane would be grateful enough to give you almost anything you might fancy. It is possible, Miss Yorke, that you might fancy Dane himself."

"That's almost funny," Sally said with a smile. "Dane will marry whom and when he wants to. Nothing but his own inclinations will influence him. When do you leave Shiran, mademoiselle?"

"I have been here four weeks; there are still five weeks of my contract at Le Perroquet, and then I go to Casablanca for a month." She paused. "You are thinking, no doubt, that as yet I have no need to concern myself about you?"

"You need never concern yourself about me," said Sally disarmingly.

"But I take no risks." Cécile's expression was bland. "I am sorry for poor Mike, but I feel he would be safer in the hands of an older, uglier nurse. Also, it seems only fair that someone old and more experienced, someone who is ready for retirement on the bounty of Dane Ryland, should be chosen to give Mike the help he needs."

Sally looked at the woman, found her oddly inscrutable. "I'm a little dense tonight," she said. "Do you mind speaking more plainly?"

"I think you understand me very well, Miss Yorke. Against you, personally, I have nothing at all. Also, I was in favour of Dane's advertising for a physiotherapist in England. Please believe those two facts."

"Very well. I believe them."

"*Bien*. It happens that you are young, you have a good English complexion and pretty hair. You are too slim for beauty and if you were a visitor here, a tourist, Dane would smile at you and forget you; that is his habit with young female guests of the hotel. But your situation is at once more intimate and more subtle. If you fail with Mike, Dane will dislike you; if you succeed, he will think there is more in you than really exists. It is human nature."

"It's a chance one is taking all the time, whatever one's profession."

"That is true, and if my home were here in Shiran, I would not count you important. However, I should prefer that you leave Shiran before I leave myself."

"Good heavens, why?"

"I have already explained. You are probably as trustworthy as any other woman, but then I do not trust women any more than I would expect them to trust me. Here in the Mirador you are in the peculiar position of being as close to Dane as you might wish, and how am I to know whether you may not desire greater closeness as the days pass?"

Cécile was breathtakingly logical; she bewildered Sally. "You're not to know, of course," she said. "I can only assure you that I'm here to work."

"Your assurance is not enough," Cécile replied sweetly. "But I would not wish you to suffer in any way. That is why I have suggested that I would introduce you to the Caid at

Nezam. He has tremendous wealth and would pay you a fabulous sum even if you could improve his son's physique only a little."

"You're actually urging me to walk out on Mike?"

"There will be someone else for him."

"But I happen to be interested in his case, and anyway, I couldn't just back out. Mr. Ryland would have a terrible opinion of me."

"You care about his opinion?" Cécile demanded.

"Yes, I do," Sally said bluntly. "He brought me over from England – paid my expenses and gave me one of the best suites in the hotel . . ."

"Which is another reason," Cécile broke in sharply, "why you should give up this job with him. He has treated you wrongly from the beginning, and you have naturally exaggerated in your mind your own importance. Anyone with your kind of training could help Mike!"

"Perhaps, but I happen to be the one who was engaged."

"You can tell Dane that you feel it is impossible for you to succeed with Mike."

"No. I wouldn't do it – not for all the money in Morocco! Quite apart from a personal pride in my job, I feel that now I've begun to help Mike I can't let up. I'd like to see the little boy you spoke about and I'd be very willing to do what I could for him, without payment, but I was engaged for Michael Ritchie and for the present he has to come first."

"So!" Patently, Cécile was astonished and displeased. "You are the first girl I have ever met who is not interested in collecting a dowry. Yet your parents cannot be rich or you would not do such exhausting work."

Unwittingly, Sally made a fatal mistake. The idea of an English girl not daring to think about marriage till she had a dowry was comic, and she laughed slightly. Cécile gave her a long penetrating glance from the dark eyes which were an unmistakable indication of her true colouring, and stood up. She had tightened like a steel spring and there was a tigerishness in her expression.

"So our customs amuse you, Miss Yorke. That is good, for you will not find much else that is funny while you are here. I was prepared to arrange this thing on a friendly basis, so that you would actually gain a good deal of money even if you lost a little of your treasured pride. But you are merely amused, and from such as you it is something I will not tolerate!"

By now, of course, Sally was distressed. "I'm terribly sorry, mademoiselle. I didn't mean to offend you. Surely you've smiled occasionally at English customs? We're a very odd race."

But Cécile was not to be mollified. "Will you do as I ask – give up this task with Michael Ritchie in favour of far better financial prospects with the Caid?"

"I'm afraid I can't."

Sally waited uneasily for an ultimatum that did not come. Cécile's curved lips became a thin line, the thick dark lashes came down over glittering eyes and the Frenchwoman turned and walked, with grace and without haste, from the suite.

Sally let out a long breath which must have been imprisoned for some time. Puzzled and apprehensive, she slipped the catch across on the outer door and went through to her bedroom, where she undressed, automatically and full of thought.

On the face of things, Cécile's reasoning was fantastic. She had gone along with Dane for two or three years, meeting no competition or at least well able to handle any that came her way. She knew herself beautiful and desirable, could probably have married well a dozen times in the past few years, and yet only a few minutes ago she had spoken as if she regarded Sally Yorke as a rival!

Sally got up from the chair where she had been peeling off her tights and took a look at her features. Fairly regular but small-boned, a pleasant whole, but that was all. And her figure hadn't a fraction of the allure of Cécile's – too gangling and countrified. What had got into the woman?

Sally analysed and reflected, shook her head. Innocently, she had overlooked one important detail. Cécile was thirty-one –

ten years older than the girl from England who might do quite a lot to earn Dane's gratitude.

For a few days Sally's life was quiet, her visits to Mike Ritchie just a little rewarding. Mike had tied himself into such tight knots that loosening off was a slow and painful process, but there came a morning when he smiled at Sally in spite of himself, and the following morning he agreed to see Tony de Chalain; the first meeting between the two young men was rather strained, but that particular fence had been surmounted.

Then, only the day after that, Sally came upon Mike sitting in his bougainvillaea-entwined veranda, and he was wearing khaki shorts and a silk shirt. This was a departure indeed. It meant that Mike was at last willing to have Sally look at his leg.

But she sat beside him without glancing at it, dropped her white straw hat on the floor at her side and breathed in the scents of almond trees and mimosa, of Damascus roses and ginger blossom.

"Mmmm. This is a sweet place, Mike. I like it better than any other part of Shiran." She paused. "I'd like to drive through the medina, but I understand it's better to do it with an escort. How about going with me?"

If he was startled, it showed only in the few seconds he allowed to elapse before replying, "Tomorrow, maybe. Don't bring anyone else."

"All right, it's a date." Sally cloaked her jubilation with a request. "May I have some lemonade?"

"Of course. I told Yussef to bring out the cool drinks the moment you arrived, but he seems to have sloped off."

"I'll get them."

He was suddenly bad-tempered, and gave the cane table a shove. "No, stay where you are." Then he yelled. "Yussef!" There was no answer and he thrust himself up on to his good leg and reached for the bell on the wall.

But before his thumb could press, he began to slide on the

tiled floor, and there was nothing to hold on to. Sally slipped under his raised arm to support him, smiled into his angry face.

"Lesson One," she said. "Don't do anything swiftly, or when you're in a temper. Keep your stick handy and make sure that the rubber tip is always in new condition."

He sank back into his chair, breathing heavily. "Damn everything," he said bitterly. "You don't know how tired of myself I am!"

"I think I do," she said softly and cheerfully. "It's just something to live through, Mike – not so bad as losing someone you love. Do you ever think of that girl?"

"No, never."

"Good; you couldn't have cared for her very much." She looked at the fleshless leg in its neat khaki stocking, saw the stark kneecap. "Do you still get pins and needles?"

"Sometimes."

"How does it feel when you're in bed?"

"It doesn't, but I get an ache in the thigh."

"That's a good sign. I'd like to give you half an hour's massage twice a day, and get you into the swimming pool every afternoon."

"Not the pool," he said abruptly.

"We could find that lagoon Dane told me about."

"I know it quite well." He shoved back the usual untidy lock of reddish hair, and asked offhandedly, "What sort of treatments do you have at your Orthopaedic Home?"

"We have hydrotherapy tanks – they're just large enough for children to splash about in, wearing an inflated tube. Then we have the jet pulsator bath – a controlled mixture of air and water played at pressure on to the affected parts. There are walking chairs for toddlers, a gym room fixed up with all kinds of gadgets. Some patients need mud baths and electrotherapy; others need to be kept happy and well while their legs are in irons and growing strong. There are steel bars everywhere, to encourage patients to use their limbs. You see, when a limb doesn't work, the rest of the body has to be extra

66

fit, so that plenty of good blood is pumped around. I had a little girl with a spinal injury . . ."

"All right," he said brusquely.

She was silent for a moment. Then: "You know, Mike, your attitude makes everything more difficult for yourself and for me. Before your accident you were such an aboundingly healthy creature that now you find yourself growing ashamed, which is a natural reaction, but awfully silly."

"If it had been a war injury or the result of a plane crash," he said jerkily, "I wouldn't care. I just went mad in a new car and smashed myself up. It was puerile!"

"Very well, so it was, but it's over. You'd soon forget it if you could walk."

His chin went stubborn. "Can you promise me I'll walk normally again?"

"No. As a matter of fact I don't think you will, and your leg won't put on much flesh, either. After treatment, you'll probably have a thinnish leg and a limp, but you'll be able to drive a car and do your job." She smiled at him mischievously. "And you'll have the girls all over you. They're sunk when they meet a handsome red-haired male with a limp."

Mike didn't smile. He sighed. "You can try massage, if you like, but it won't work any wonders."

Sally dropped a cushion on the tiles and sat on it; she rolled down his sock. The leg was pale, except where a purple scar ran behind the knee, but Sally had seen worse. This leg might have looked almost normal on a thin man. Her sensitive fingers held the calf muscle, squeezed here and there, and discovered by faint movement that he felt it slightly.

In a voice quite different from his usual one, he asked, "Are you my kind of girl, Sally? Or am I just The Leg to you?"

Sally gave these queries the interest they deserved. "I don't think I'm your kind of girl – not quite. And you're not The Leg to me. I haven't really thought much about your leg till this morning; there seemed to be so much else to think about first. I hope that now you've forgiven me for coming, we're going to be friends."

"If I refuse to go to England for treatment but am willing to do whatever you want right here in Shiran, will you stick by me till I can walk a little?"

"I think I can promise that, Mike – unless Dane sends me away."

"He can't do that!"

He stopped speaking and watched the road. The car he had glimpsed turned on to the drive and purred round to the foot of the steps. It halted and the door opened.

"Speak of the omnipotent," said Mike under his breath.

Sally stayed very still, watching Dane as he took the steps in one stride and came lazily along to where they sat. Then she stopped watching him, because she was still seated on the cushion and he was a mile above her.

"Hallo there," he said nonchalantly. "Mind my joining you? I'm on my way to look at a proposition and thought I'd call in. You two look cosy."

"Sally's just taken her first sight of my leg. She wasn't horrified."

"Nothing in the least unpleasant about it," commented Sally. She touched Mike's knee lightly with her forefinger. "There's probably a fibrous stiffening of the joint that needs ordinary massage, but otherwise the prescription will be regulated exercise of different kinds. I'll have to take Mike's X-rays along to Dr. Demaire and get his instructions."

"Demaire!" exclaimed Mike. "He's a g.p."

"I don't suppose you have a local medical man who's qualified in physiotherapy, have you?"

"Demaire's pretty good and he's studied Mike's case," said Dane. "See him by all means, Sally. You might get him out here to see Mike, as well."

"Oh, no. No more doctors!" Mike rested an arm on the table. "I'll have what Sally can give or nothing at all."

"I'm not supposed to work without a doctor," she said lightly.

"All right. See Demaire, but don't bring him here."

Dane said decisively, "You're being a fool, Mike. Let's

wade into this business and get your leg as near right as we can, without delay. You've messed about long enough."

Mike's chin stuck out, obstinately. "I'm not going to be pushed around. I've said I'll let Sally have a go at it, and I will, but I won't have you and Demaire bossing me while she's about it. I know I owe you more than I can ever repay . . ."

"Shut up. The really big debt you owe is to yourself. Get up on your legs and use them. If you need someone to lean on, I'm right here in Shiran, and you can call me at any time. For Pete's sake stop pitying yourself and get cracking!"

Sally said hurriedly, but pacifically, "There's no need for heat. Mike, tell me where I can find your hospital file and I'll fetch it now."

"I'll get it," said Dane, and he stalked into the house.

Mike glanced down at Sally's bronze hair and said a little breathily, "If Dane weren't so darned healthy himself, he might understand. I believe he's beginning to wish he'd never brought you here."

Sally considered this for an instant. "You may be right, but it doesn't make any difference. I'm here for as long as you need me. But promise me something. Don't quarrel with Dane. He wants to see you debonair and taking your pick of the girls again. Please don't quarrel with him."

There was no time for more. Dane appeared, carrying a fibre-board file which seemed to be full of X-ray films and papers. He reached a negligent hand down to Sally, pulled her to her feet, and said pleasantly, "I think Sally might as well see Demaire today, if it can be arranged. Either she or I will let you know the result this evening, Mike. We'll push off now."

"Sally, too?"

"She may as well. See you later."

Sally gathered her hat, smiled at Mike and felt herself pushed firmly but gently down the steps to the path. Dane called to the driver of the car which had brought her, and told him he would be driving mademoiselle himself. Sally was put into the front seat of the silver and blue affair and Dane set it moving. They waved to Mike, who made no attempt to wave back, and slipped out on to the road, turning uphill away from Shiran.

"You've upset your cousin," said Sally crossly. "Why do you do it?"

"Someone has to keep Mike's feet on the ground," Dane answered calmly, "or he'll lose sight of the reason you're here." He paused. "Nice work, Sally."

"What was?"

"The little-girl pose, kneeling at his feet. What comes next – your head against his knee, and family reminiscences?"

Sally was angry but determined not to show it. "Does it matter? You want Mike to get back his interest in life and I'm trying my hardest, in the only way I know, to see that you get your money's worth. It's taken me eight solid days to get Mike's confidence, and you had to walk in and do your best to shatter the whole thing!"

"Oh, come. Mike knows me. He probably thinks I browbeat you as well."

"And you do!"

"Not really; with you I only play at it. You're not difficult to manage."

"Is that contempt or flattery?"

"I'm afraid it's only the truth. Not that I don't think you could be damned difficult if you were given your head . . . or if your feelings became involved. You're probably the type who'd defend her patients and adorers to the death."

"Oh, go climb a tree!"

He laughed briefly. "I'm your employer . . . remember?"

"I don't work for an employer. I work for the patient and the doctor. Do you know what Mike thinks? He believes you're sorry you brought me here."

Oddly, this created a silence.

"Did I let slip a brick of some kind?" she asked.

"Nothing bigger than you've dropped before, little one," he said non-committally. "In some ways you're so uninhibited that you take me by surprise. If I were sorry you're here, I'd send you away."

"I doubt if you could, you know. I'm almost sure that, if you tried it, Mike would take me on himself."

"When you're a resident here, as I am, it's quite easy to arrange for a visa to be withdrawn. Not that I'd do it to you," very coolly, "but just don't start talking about transferring your allegiance."

"I didn't mean it that way. What I was getting at, really, was that I'm beginning to feel that Mike is my job, and I do like to see a job right through. At times, during the past week, I've had a glimpse of the sort of person Mike was before his accident. He must have been great fun."

"But his motto was love 'em and leave 'em. Remember that."

"That's true of half the men one meets. I think in that direction Mike will be different in future. There's nothing like losing the things you value for a while to give you a true perspective on things that matter."

"Pint-size wisdom," he said mockingly, but his fleeting glance at her was sharp. "As soon as Mike responds to treatment you'll have to abandon the sugary tactics. Go professional on him."

She smiled. "Very well, sir. I'm well up in self-defence."

"It won't be in the least funny if he falls for you."

"Of course not; it'll be touching, but nothing to worry about. Actually, our best bet would be to have a girl ready for him – someone really fetching."

He grinned. "You're a sane child, Sally Yorke. I wonder if you'll be as wise over your own affairs of the heart?"

"I hope so," she said apprehensively. "I want my love affair to be one of those certain things in life – smooth from the beginning and lovelier every day. Are they ever like that?"

"They are – for cold fish."

"How do I discover whether I'm a cold fish?"

He sounded bantering, but the faint sharpness still edged his tones. "You experiment, little one. If I kissed you, I could tell you straight away."

Sally's eyes widened, and she stared rather hard at the yellow

71

road ahead. "Bit drastic, though, isn't it? How would you know?"

"If you hated it, you'd fight. If you liked it, you might still fight, but in a different way. If you were a cold fish, you'd break it off just as it became interesting, look at me sweetly and say 'That was nice'."

A tremor of laughter ran through her. "You blind me with your experience. If I ever go in for experiment I'll do it with someone my own weight."

"Tony?" he asked casually.

"Why not?" she replied lightly. "At least he wouldn't treat me as a piece of research, or get too serious. Falling in love is a grave business, but I think the approach to it should be gay."

"That's the farmhouse wench in you," he said tersely. "You were reared on gambolling lambs and dancing grass. On the whole, it might be best for you to save your first love affair till you get back to England."

It was strange, but in that moment Sally knew a sudden ache of knowledge – that she hated the lightness with which he was able to regard her as a temporary acquaintance. Hated it more, because she felt certain that he took a peculiar pleasure in reminding her of her own impermanence here in Shiran.

"Where are we going?" she asked offhandedly.

He accepted the change of topic without comment. "I promised Pierre that I'd look at the date plantation Tony's keen on. It wouldn't be fair to turn down the proposition completely without seeing the place first. Thought you might like to go along."

"Yes, I would. I've never seen a date plantation."

"You've never seen a kasbah, either. I have an invitation to bring a party of Europeans to a function in a kasbah next week. Care to be one of us?"

"Why, yes, I'd love it!"

"Good. No special dress, except that your dress must be high at the neck." Then: "How much have you found out about Tony?"

"There's not a lot to find out, is there? He was educated in

72

England, came back to Morocco and couldn't settle in a job. If Monsieur de Chalain had married again, he might not have spoiled Tony."

"So you don't think it's wrong of Pierre to consider bankrupting himself in order to give Tony the plantation he wants?"

"That's difficult to answer. Tony thinks that with you holding the reins, the plantation would be sure to succeed. If it did, his father would get his money back, plus interest."

"You're gullible, young Sally. Tony's convinced you that he has staying power. Mike used to like good times and plenty of money to throw about, but he was quick and thorough at his job. Tony's only a few months younger and he's never even picked on a career, let alone worked at it."

"But the difference between them proves something, don't you see?" she protested quickly. "Tony could get what he liked from his father, and each time he failed at something he was excused and helped. Mike had you, not a sentimental parent."

"Don't give me that," he said scoffingly. "Mike had it in him. Tony's just a nice-looking parasite."

"If you like Pierre," she said firmly, "you'll try to convert Tony."

"I've enough on my hands. Tony's twenty-six and old enough to think for himself. At his age I was managing a trading company."

"You probably started managing something or someone the moment you were born!" she returned warmly. "Haven't you any sympathy at all with the weak?"

He glanced at her in mild astonishment. "Not a lot, when the weakness is Tony's type. You haven't been here much more than a week. Why should you care whether I help Tony?"

Sally couldn't explain. She lifted her shoulders. "It's not my concern, is it? Tell me about the countryside."

After a few moments, he did. They passed sudden gulfs and chasms, and plantations of cork oaks, where strippers were peeling bark which looked like watered silk. There were forests of argan trees where goats wandered, not only on the ground but high among the gnarled branches, nibbling the new green shoots and stepping daintily among the twigs in search of more. The car had to slow down for a camel-train which was making for a distant kasbah with loads of spices and silks and leather, and then they came to a sandier soil, where strange mauve and scarlet flowers grew among wild olives and rough tan-coloured rocks.

Sally looked at Dane, noticed a little vexedly that he appeared serene. He was at home in this country; the desert and the glitter, the fine-looking dark-skinned people, the very spirit of the country, had got into him, and he had made them his own.

Sally took off the sun-glasses and looked across the palms to the mountains. The light was brilliant and searing, the shadows a curious purple. There were no half-tones or hints of pastel, just as there was nothing muted about the population; the Moors were either very rich and educated or so poor that they had to barter and beg.

At a lane which led through to a decaying white house, Dane pulled in. "This is it," he said. "Tony's pipe-dream."

"There seem to be a good many dead palms," she commented.

"Disease of some sort; they don't often die from lack of water."

"The place could be put right, though, couldn't it?"

Dane nodded, meditatively. "Out with the dead wood and in with new, plenty of pruning, and so on. It wouldn't cost the earth, but Tony's too irresponsible to see it through."

"Not if he were watched."

"I haven't time to watch him." He opened his door. "Let's look at the house."

They walked along the lane in the blanketing heat, went up into a narrow veranda. Dane produced a key and opened the door into a mosaic-floored room which had lost several tiles and was thick with sand and dust. Opposite the entrance, a flight of dirty marble steps led to the bedrooms, and after a cursory glance about him Dane nodded upwards.

74

"Shall we investigate? May as well weigh up the cost of repairs, now we're here."

"Does that mean you're seriously considering the plantation?" she queried eagerly.

"It means I'm keeping my word," he answered sourly. "I promised to look the place over, and I will."

They mounted the stairs, turned a corner and came to a landing on to which all the upper rooms opened. The doors stood wide, and Dane chose the nearest room, a large one with a peeling balcony which looked way over the tops of the palms to a distant lilac line of mountains. Sally stared, entranced, and Dane came behind her and took in the scene.

"Well, what do you think of the vista?" he asked. "Another stock scene?"

She shook her bronze head. "It's fascinating. It may sound crazy, but this seems far more real than the esplanade at Shiran. If I lived here and there were plenty of water, I'd force some grass and flowers to grow round the house."

"Really?" He was cool for some reason. "And what would you do with the house itself – blow it down and build again or patch it up with Sellotape?"

"Are you always contemptuous of ideas and plans that aren't your own?"

"I guess I've developed a bad mood."

She looked at him quickly. "Through me?"

He drew in his lip and smiled cynically. "Don't make something of it, little one. Let's get out of this house before it falls about our ears."

"I think it's solid enough. Is this the balcony over the front door?"

She didn't wait for his answer, but went to the wall and leaned over the cracking plaster. In the next second she felt her hand give way and heard Dane's exclamation. What happened then she never clearly recalled. There was the crashing sound and the sudden sensation of completely losing balance, the clatter of more dislodged masonry on the earth below. But she never quite worked out how she had slipped

75

and found herself dangling in air, with Dane flat on the balcony floor and gripping her with excruciating tightness about the ribs. His chin was the first thing she became aware of; it was boring a groove into her forehead.

"Keep quite still," he said in quiet, taut tones. "The rest of this balcony could collapse at any moment. Go as limp as you can and leave things to me. For heaven's sake don't try to help."

"I won't," she whispered, and because of the pain of his grip she closed her eyes.

Practically the whole of the balcony wall had gone, leaving jagged edges of brick and stucco which, somehow, he had to keep away from her thinly-clad body as he inched her upwards, and himself slid back into the room. With one arm taking her weight, he used his other hand as a shield, first to her ribs and then to her waist and thigh. The dress ripped in several places, it got in his way and he cursed it under his breath, but in the final stage it helped him because he was able to bunch it and lift her the rest of the way in one go. A couple of minutes later he had dragged them both into the room, and released her.

Bruised and shaken, Sally lay on her side with her face turned into her arm. She heard his hard mechanical breathing and forced herself to rise on an elbow and look at him. What she saw drove the blood from her heart.

His eyes blazed, white-hot, like bits of steel in a furnace. His teeth were so tight that muscles stood out in the lean jaws, and the hand he leant back upon was clenched whitely into a fist that looked as though it would drive straight through the stone floor.

"You . . . idiot," he breathed. "You could have landed on your head and been killed."

"I'm sorry," she whispered.

Her hair had fallen forward and the blue eyes were huge with remembered fright. She gazed at him and her lips trembled, and with a savage movement he shoved an arm round her and pushed back her hair.

"All right, Sally." His voice was more normal. "You had a shock and so did I. Wait a bit, before you move."

There was a silence, during which she became acutely conscious of his arm about her and his breath on her forehead. She stirred, let out a shuddering sigh and felt his arm tighten, lifted her head and found her face close to his; his eyes were still smouldering. For a long moment of blank intensity she was entirely without volition; dazedly she knew that her mouth moved a fraction closer to his, but only because he had first lowered his head. She quivered, and he let her go, abruptly.

He spoke in cool, sarcastic tones. "That's what emotion does for you. You get stirred up over something and before you know it you're back on the old routine. Are you hurt anywhere?"

Was she hurt! Her whole nervous system was in shreds. But she shook her head. "I don't know how to thank you, Dane. I'm afraid your hand came off badly . . ."

"Forget it." He stood up, and his grip on her elbow as he helped her to her feet was hard and impersonal. Without haste, they went out on to the landing and down the stairs. As he walked, Dane wound a handkerchief about his hand and tucked in the ends. He pulled the door shut behind them and tested the lock, guided her round the fallen debris. They walked to the car and he set it in motion.

He drove fast, without speaking. Sally wondered, hollowly, if he was thinking how near he had come to discovering whether she were a cold fish. She felt sick and full of foreboding, had the horrid conviction that if she did not leave Shiran at once she would regret it for ever. Yet something held her here in Morocco, something far stronger than anything she had ever imagined could exist.

Dust swirled behind them, landmarks leapt up to meet them. Only an hour after leaving the plantation they were curving round the drive of the Hotel Mirador. Sally was helped out on to the tiled courtyard, she reached back into the car for her wide-brimmed hat and held it in front of her to conceal the most blatant rip in her dress. Dane gripped her arm with angry fingers, led her up into the foyer.

"I'll send up some lunch," he said, in glacial syllables, "and you'd better lie down as soon as you've had it. Go straight into the lift.''

A pyramid of dashing and very feminine blue and white travelling bags stood near the lift, and the reception clerk was gesticulating excitedly to Pierre de Chalain. Someone, apparently, was demanding the best suite in the hotel, and no suites of any kind were available.

Sally entered the lift and was wafted upwards. She walked the silent corridor to her room and opened the door. Sanctuary, she thought thankfully, as she entered the air-conditioned coolness of the sitting-room.

And then she stopped, precipitately, and stared at the exquisite young woman who awaited her. She had the aquiline features of a well-bred Latin, night-black hair, an olive skin and the figure of a dancer. Her thin black suit was the latest thing from Paris, very narrow and elegant, but her smile had nothing tailored about it; it was brilliant and spontaneous.

"Sally!" A hearty hug. "Oh, Sally, it's so good to see you!"

"Lucette," said Sally faintly, "Why, Lucette!"

CHAPTER FIVE

Too many things were happening at once for Sally. The greeting over, she leaned back upon the table and tried to sort this particular moment from the rest of the morning. Lucette Millar was here, twice as large as life! Those were her bags downstairs. Dozens of them. And Lucette was talking with her usual lack of restraint.

"It was so strange, Sally. Your letter arriving while my parents were out for a few hours. I took in the mail and there it was – just what I'd been waiting for! Darling, you don't know how I felt. I gathered, of course, that you'd been writing fairly often, and knew my mother must have destroyed anything in your handwriting. She read your letters before burning them – you can be sure of that! I was infuriated – almost gave myself away when my parents got in that evening. But somehow I hung on to my temper, and next day I started planning. And here I am!"

"But how did you manage it? I though they never let you out of Tangier."

The black glance evaded Sally's, and Lucette laughed. "It was easy, once I knew where to come. You couldn't have chosen a better place. They'll never think to look for me here." She paused anxiously. "You didn't write again, did you, Sally? There won't be a letter giving the show away?"

"No. No, I didn't write again." Dazedly, Sally realized that since posting the one letter she had hardly thought of Lucette. "That luggage downstairs . . . how long are you staying?"

"For days and days. And what do you think? They say they haven't a suite for me! I told them nothing less would do and left them sorting it out." She looked about her. "I like this. They're doing you proud, Sally."

It was unbelievable, but Sally felt she would have given any-

79

thing to remain alone in the suite. However, she had to say, "You can share it if you like. There's a huge bedroom with twin beds."

"Marvellous! I couldn't wish for anything better." Lucette got up from her chair and dropped a long snakeskin purse on the table, took off her little black cap and stretched her arms rapturously. "This freedom! You have to be imprisoned before you can appreciate it. Oh, Sally, you don't know how I feel – so happy and full of life. I'm going to have the best time in the world!"

"You still haven't explained how you got away from Tangier. You've brought so much luggage that your parents must have known all about it."

"Oh, they knew – but not where I was bound for. I put on labels for Casablanca and had them changed at the airport."

"But why should they let you go to Casablanca?"

Lucette said gaily, "Because I have a very solemn relative there, darling, and I've been there before, without dire consequences."

"But won't they get in touch with your relative?"

"No. You're probably aware that the plane from Tangier stops at Casablanca, and I sent them a telegram from there to say I'd arrived. It was that simple!"

"But if you stay away for long they'll expect letters."

"Not from Lucette – she's a bad girl who's gone all independent since . . . well, since she's been twenty-one. I'm twenty-two next week, you know."

"Yes, I remember." Sally paused, and pushed a hand over her brow. "What about that old man they were trying to make you marry?"

Lucette looked startled, as if she could not quite recollect having written such words. "He was not so old, but it's all been dealt with. I will tell you about it some time." Quickly, rather more quickly than was necessary, Sally thought, she changed the subject. "Tell me what you do here. Have you met any exciting men?"

"Not your sort of exciting. I'm here to work."

"Pooh to that. We'll have fun, lots of it." She sighed gustily with pure pleasure. "This is bliss. I'm free, and with my sweetie Sal. How are your brothers?"

It was typical of Lucette that she should enquire first about the young men and only then put a polite query about Mr. and Mrs. Yorke, who had made her welcome so many times as a schoolgirl.

"They were fine when I left England," said Sally. "I'm afraid Geoff got over his crush on you."

"Never mind – it was a long time and many crushes ago. Your respected mother and father are still wearing tweeds and reading *Farmer's Weekly*, I suppose?"

"They always will, thank goodness." Sally was recovering a little, and discovering that Lucette's fingers and wrists were rather plentifully encircled with jewellery. "Have you been left a fortune, or something?"

"These?" Lucette jiggled her hands. "All phoney, darling." She nodded at Sally's dress. "Your patient seems to be rather violent. Do you have to handle him alone?"

Sally summoned a smile. "I had an accident. Mind if I change right away? If you want to go on talking I shall be able to hear you in the bedroom."

But Lucette followed her, taking off a couple of bracelets and a ring or two and slipping them into a drawer. She was left wearing a gold wristlet which must have weighed half a pound and a diamond ring on each hand. The jewellery, she explained, had been left her by a grandmother; she had worn it all because it was safer than packing it; it had sentimental value only, of course, but she didn't want to lose it. Sally handed over the key to the drawer, and then washed and got into a clean dress. She used powder and lipstick, brushed her hair and felt better.

They had just returned to the sitting-room when a knock came at the door and a servant wheeled in a luncheon trolley. And straight behind the trolley came Dane, looking as fresh and nonchalant as if he had spent the morning down at the pool. He did glance rather keenly at Sally, but after that he wore the sort of smile that ties feminine hearts in knots, and his tones were lazily interested.

"Mr. Ryland . . . Miss Millar," said Sally carefully. "Lucette and I were at school together."

"Really?" said Dane, appraising Lucette's dark, vital features. "I'm charmed to know you, Miss Millar. I hear you're expecting a suite all to yourself."

Lucette's pleased surprise at encountering such a man within the first hour of her arrival was openly intense. "Not now. You see, I didn't know that Sally would have such a magnificent flat all to herself. We've decided to share."

"That's fine. Knowing you were here with Miss Yorke, I took the liberty of adding a bottle of champagne to the luncheon. With the hotel's compliments."

"What a lovely gesture!" exclaimed Lucette, scintillating for all she was worth. "Won't you open the bottle, Mr. Ryland, and drink with us?"

Mr. Ryland did, somehow managing to keep hidden the hand which had adhesive plaster over the knuckles. He bowed as he raised his glass, made a few suave remarks, finished his drink and left them. The door closed with an insidious quietness, and Sally was aware of an ache where he had gripped her about the ribs. But Lucette was enchanted.

"He's mine," she said, whirling about with the empty glass aloft. "And you said there were no men!"

"I said *your* kind of men. Dane Ryland doesn't buckle at the knees at the sight of a pretty girl."

"Maybe not, but he didn't get that charm of his through sticking to male company. He's a dream!"

"He's anything but," replied Sally with a trace of acid. "And there's a woman who has first claim. You may have heard of her. Cécile Vaugard?"

"The singing siren? I've seen her in Tangier."

"Does she know you?"

"Oh, no. She was in some operatic thing I had to sit through once." Lucette was sobered. "She was quite a looker."

"The most beautiful woman I've ever seen."

"Blonde?"

82

"Honey-fair, with dark eyes."

"And the Dane man goes for her?"

"She's the only woman he takes about in Shiran."

"Depressing, isn't it?" But Lucette instantly brightened. "I'll try for him all the same." She examined the silver dishes on the trolley. "I suppose, being thin and energetic, you can eat this delicious stuff without bothering about your figure? I'll take some salad and a roll."

As it happened, Sally wasn't a bit hungry. She ate a little, talked a little and listened a great deal. Lucette, she decided, had not changed very much. She was still volatile and merry, seldom cast down about anything for longer than a minute. She, Sally, ought to have remembered Lucette's temperament when she had received the letter full of utter misery back in England. Somehow, Lucette either wriggled out of everything unpleasant, or she changed her views and came to like the bugbear. She was mercurial, full of stratagems and little tricks, fond of money and fun but basically loyal.

Sally's mother had always blamed the Millar parents for the oddities in Lucette's character. They were both English with a dash of Latin and distinctly bohemian in outlook, and Mr. Millar had had one of those convenient arty jobs which allowed him to live almost anywhere and conduct his business by mail. The Millars had never settled anywhere for more than three or four years, and it was quite possible that they would soon uproot themselves once more and glide along to the other end of the Mediterranean.

Perhaps it was natural that, living mostly in southern Europe or the northern tip of Africa, they should have strict ideas about their daughter while she lived with them. They had even gone to the length of trying to make her marry someone they had chosen for her, but Lucette, apparently, had successfully jibbed. Well, it wouldn't do her any harm to be away from them for a while.

Sally said presently, "I still don't understand what's been happening to you, Lucette. You were so keen to run away from home – and you hadn't any money of your own. Yet you've arrived here by air, and presumably you have enough money to pay for a luxury suite."

"Actually," Lucette confided, "I sold something. It's sort of pawned, really, because I can get it back if I ever have enough cash. In Tangier you can find people who'll accommodate you with money so long as the security is about fifteen times greater than the sum you want. But don't let's be sordid, darling. I have to make the most of this break!"

"Some time it will become known that you didn't stay in Casablanca. Have you decided how you'll explain it away to your parents?"

"No, but I've plenty of time to hit on some watertight idea, and you can help me manufacture something really plausible. I've never been able to live in anything but the present. You know that."

Yes, Sally knew it. She could remember two days of black anxiety when Lucette had been a member of the Yorke household, two long nights when the whole family had searched the hills and worried. Lucette had cheerfully turned up at noon on the third day, after a riotous sojourn with a group of girl and boy cycle tourists from Holland. There was never any need to worry about her, Lucette had protested; life was so glum if you couldn't do just as you wished when the fit took you.

It seemed she still cherished the same philosophy, but she was grown up now, and likely to cause a different kind of trouble. However, Sally realized there was nothing on earth she herself could do about it. Lucette was of age, and if her accounts of her parents' strictness was true, it was time she had some freedom. But unaccountably Sally wished her friend had not come to Shiran. She decided to escape.

"I have to see the doctor about Mike Ritchie," she said. "I'll be back later."

"Oh, that's all right," was the airy reply. "I'll find my way about and make a few friends. Don't hurry for me."

Her emotions jumbled, Sally went down to the vestibule and asked the reception clerk to telephone Dr. Demaire's residence for an appointment. She was told that the doctor was resting after lunch, and she could call at any time within the next half-hour. When, twenty minutes later, she was shown into an old-fashioned French drawing-room in one of the crowded houses on the Avenue Lyautey, Sally found that the doctor was already in possession of Mike's file, and ready to prescribe his physiotherapy. When she left him she felt that at last she was in command, and on an impulse she changed her instructions to the driver.

"Take me up to Monsieur Ritchie's house, please."

By the time she was walking up into Mike's porch, Sally's head was beginning to throb. She pressed the bell and walked in, took off her hat and turned to greet Mike as he wheeled himself into the room.

"Hallo," she said. "We've fixed everything. Exercises every morning, a swim in the afternoon and a spot of massage every evening to break up the adhesions."

He smiled wearily. "Sounds like a full-time job for you."

"It's nothing, really. Only half an hour each time, and if you'd rather swim with a man, you may. I suggest we get Tony along and find the lagoon each day for a few days. After that, you'll be able to manage on the beach here in Shiran, or even at the Mirador pool. Then you need only see me twice a day, on professional business."

"What makes you think I don't want to see you otherwise?"

"Well, in a way I hope you will," she said. "Only . . . don't get a sort of fixation for me, Mike. It's awfully common, you know – patient falling for the nurse if she's at all presentable, particularly in private cases."

His face looked thinner, his hazel eyes darker. "Don't you like me much?"

"I like you immensely."

"I'm glad your friendliness hasn't been all tactics," he said bitterly. "I'm not at all sure I want to go on with this therapy stuff."

"Mike." She came to him, shook him gently, chidingly. "I'm just a girl who's been trained to help people like you. You don't have to see me as the ideal woman as well. Once you're on your feet you'll soon discover that I'm anything but perfect, and you'll start looking about you for someone prettier and more accommodating." She smiled suddenly. "As a matter of fact, I've just the wench for you – arrived today! She's a friend of mine – terribly attractive, lively, full of sex appeal, joie de vivre and what have you. She always stuns the men."

"I'm past it," he said briefly.

"I'll believe that if you say it again in six months' time! How about taking a walk with me?"

"Now?"

"Right now. I'll get your sticks." She collected them from the corner of his bedroom, came back and put the normal one into his right hand. The other she strapped above his left elbow. "Put the brake on the chair and get up on to your right foot with your arm round my shoulder. That's it. Now let's get this other contraption working in your left hand. Better than the old crutch, isn't it?"

"Slightly. It's hell on the arms."

"We'll have to massage those, too," she said, almost happy now that she was really working on him. "I'll go first and you follow about a pace behind. If you feel at all uncertain just make a grab at me. I'll be ready to take your weight. Swing that leg from the hip – from the knee, too, if you can. All right?"

They reached the porch, turned gently along the veranda, where she said lightly, "You can rest here for a bit," and plumped up a cushion.

But she didn't help him down on to the canvas chair, and she let him arrange the sticks himself.

"You see?" she said. "You don't have to use the servant at all. You can do it all alone. Just make him walk in front, as I did."

"I feel as if I've climbed a mountain."

"You will, for a while, but it will be a smaller mountain each time. The morning exercises will soon get you into fine condition, and then the whole thing will be easier."

He lay back, pushed at his long hair. "It's going to be the deuce of a long job, though, isn't it?"

"Afraid so. In hospital, with medicated baths and so on, you'd be through much quicker ..."

"I'm not leaving Morocco!"

"We know that," she said soothingly. "That's why we're doing the long-term stuff. Would you like a cup of tea?"

"Ring the bell and order it. How long can you stay?"

"As long as you need me."

His eyelids flickered and he got out a box of cigarettes. "That's a funny answer. I need you all the time."

"Not me, particularly. You've been too long without company. Does Tony come to see you?"

He nodded, and offered the cigarettes. "He's got dates on the brain. I've never known him so keen on anything before."

She bent her cigarette to the match he held, blew smoke. "I went to the date plantation this morning, with Dane."

"You did?" He was watching her curiously. "Why did he take you?"

"Goodness knows. He didn't enjoy it and neither did I."

A brief silence. Then he asked casually, "Was it Dane who told you to put me in my place next time you saw me?"

She hesitated, and thereby told him more than she intended. "He's as much against complications as I am. As soon as you get feeling into that leg of yours you'll be so grateful that it won't be wise to trust your emotions. It may sound all very silly ..."

"It doesn't; it sounds sense. The trouble is, I'm fed to the gills with wisdom. I want to go haywire."

"You do that – but not just yet."

The tea came and she poured it out. As usual, it was mint tea, and she drank it reluctantly, from a glass. She ate one of the sweet nut pyramids and lay back in her chair, looking with some degree of contentment over the garden. Here with Mike, this morning and tomorrow seemed remote; she knew a sensation of isolation from the Mirador, and was glad.

She talked idly, and waited till five-thirty before she got up to go. "I won't come tonight," she said. "We'll start away on the full day's treatment tomorrow. Like to go indoors?"

"No, thanks. I'll stay here till the sun goes. Make it nine-thirty tomorrow morning."

"Ten o'clock," she said.

"Nine-thirty!"

She smiled and compromised. "A quarter to ten. And I'll ask Tony to go with us to the lagoon in the afternoon." She touched his hand, lightly. "We're on our way, Mike. This time next year you'll be driving again!"

She said goodbye and went down to the car. The driver sprang up from his cross-legged position on the grass and opened the door. Sally waved as they moved away. Then she leaned back in the corner of the car and knew the respite was over.

They were out on the road and gathering speed when a taxi growled past. Sally caught a glimpse of the single occupant of the back seat, turned and watched the taxi take the bend into Mike Ritchie's drive. Cécile Vaugard visiting Mike? Sally puzzled it over for a few minutes, decided that it wasn't really her business, and forgot about it.

To Sally's relief, the very next morning Dane was called to the phosphate mine for a few days. He looked in at Suite Seven at nine-fifteen, lifted a brow when he heard that Lucette was still in bed.

"That friend of yours knows a thing or two, young Sally. There's nothing like plenty of rest and a merry outlook to keep a woman young and vital. In age, she may give you only a few months, but in experience she's years ahead of you. But she doesn't carry it in her face – not noticeably, anyway."

"You're wrong about Lucette. Her parents are terribly stern," Sally answered coolly.

"I'm right," he said equably. "Her eyes occasionally give her away. Don't let her teach you too much, too soon."

He told Sally he had to go to the mine, gave her a brief

and mocking glance as he asked, "Feel any effects from yesterday?"

"No. Do you?"

"Nothing physical." His smile was narrow as he looked down at the bare, grazed knuckles of his hand. "Told anyone?"

"No."

"Just as well. Pierre assumed that I'd caught my hand on a wall somewhere. By the way, during my absence he'll probably invite you and your friend to dine with him and Tony. Go ahead and do so, if you want to."

"It's very kind of you to consent," she said stiffly.

"Not really. You see, I'm going to back the date plantation after all."

"You are? I'm so glad!"

"Thought you might be," he said coolly. "But I've made a few conditions. One of them forbids Tony to marry for two years."

Sally stared at him. "Why would you do that? His private life isn't your concern."

He shrugged, smiled a little unpleasantly. "They invited me into the proposition and those are my terms. If Tony can manage to give everything he has to the plantation for two years, he'll be set up, both financially and in his character. Incidentally, he'll make a far better husband if he denies himself a few pleasures and works instead."

"You're very hard."

"On Tony, or on you?"

"I don't come into it."

"You do," he said crisply. "You're more than half the reason I decided to support the scheme. You thought Tony should be given his chance, and upon reflection I agreed with you." His tone was suddenly metallic. "Two years will give you ample time to discover whether it's the atmosphere or Tony that gets you."

"Two years! I shan't be here that long." Then she realized the whole of what he had said, and added quickly, "I'm not falling in love with Tony."

"Then why did you argue with me about the plantation?"

"Well, he seemed sincere about it, and it's obvious that you could help him to make a success of it."

He came back at her at once. "Do you often find yourself planning a man's future after knowing him a few days?"

"This is different . . ."

"I thought so." He was taut and concise. "Let me make something very clear. Out here, you can imagine yourself in love simply because there's a kind of magnetism in the air. If I had absolutely refused to take an interest in the plantation, you'd have been all sympathy and compassion – just as you're all pity and emotion for Mike. But Tony is keen to settle and he's backed by his father. If I hadn't insisted on the no-marriage clause in the contract, he'd have been proposing to you within the next few days."

"That's absurd! There's never been anything of that kind between us."

"Because he's had nothing to offer. Pierre was disappointed when I stipulated the two years."

"And Tony?"

"He lost his smile, too. They both knew I was safeguarding you."

Sally was becoming really angry. "I don't need that sort of protection. Even if I wanted to make an impression on Tony and his father, it wouldn't be your business."

"Maybe not, but I won't have you diving into your first affair right here in the Mirador and coming to grief." His voice lowered, and he added with cool malice, "Love in these parts is suspect, and first love should always have a drab backcloth; then you know how real it is. After the first attack you're a better judge."

"Is that how . . . *you've* found it?"

"Yes, Sally. That's how I've found it. I'll have to get going."

But as he moved back towards the door the bedroom door opened and Lucette drifted in, stretching prettily and pushing pink-tipped fingers through tousled black curls. She looked drowsy and sweet in the tailored Chinese silk wrap, but her sudden smile at Dane was arch and inviting.

"Why, good morning. Were you shouting at Sally, you naughty man?"

He grinned, looked as if he couldn't help grinning; she was like an enchanting kitten. "Good morning, Miss Millar. How do you like the Mirador?"

"It's splendid . . . and so discreet. And you're rather charming, too."

"Why, thanks," he answered, with a sidelong glance at Sally. "You must tell me that again when I get back. I may be able to do something about it." Nonchalantly, he bowed to them both. "You'll excuse me now?"

He was gone, and Sally felt a lump as rough and large as a peach stone in her throat. He was beginning to hurt her in a way she had never been hurt before, and that was why it was such a relief to have him gone for a few days. Now she wouldn't have to brace herself every time she stepped out of the suite; she could relax a little, and give herself completely to the task of helping Mike.

The following days had a serenity of their own. True, Tony sought her out and complained about the cold-blooded clause in the date plantation contract, and Pierre looked both sad and happy when he invited Lucette and Sally to dine with himself and his son. But because Tony was going to get largely what he wanted, and because Lucette's shining presence enlivened most occasions, there was gaiety in their small circle.

Actually, Sally did not spend much time at the hotel. She went alone to Mike's house, supervised his exercises and got him stumping about the house and veranda, stayed to lunch sometimes, and drove with him in the afternoon to the lagoon. There they met Tony, who gave Mike his shoulder down to the water.

Mike had always been a strong swimmer and he found it almost as easy to swim with one leg as with two. After half an hour in the water they would laze under the palms, smoke a cigarette, and the two young men would swop tall yarns for Sally's benefit.

After an hour or two near the lagoon, Tony would help Mike into the car, get back into his father's ancient vehicle and lead the way homeward. Mike, a little sleepy, would lie in his corner of the back seat without speaking.

One afternoon, when they were on their way back to Shiran, Sally saw him draw the thin leg up on to the other knee and inspect it closely.

"It's getting brown," he said suddenly. "I can feel the skin burning."

Sally's heart leapt, but she answered casually, "Of course you can. What do you think we're working for?"

He was speechless for a moment. Then: "I'm coming to the Mirador for dinner tonight!"

"Wonderful. I'll send the car for you."

"You mean it's all right?"

"Of course it's all right. I haven't dined downstairs for about a week, so we'll make it a big night. And you'll meet Lucette!"

"Your friend? What does she do with herself while you're out?"

"She's as friendly as a puppy – a sophisticated one. She already knows more people at the Mirador than I do. I think you'll rather go for Lucette."

He let the leg drop and smiled disagreeably. "I go for you," he said. "That's enough for now."

"Thank you," said Sally brightly, and she left it there.

When she entered her suite at the Mirador all was quiet, and she sank into a chair and let the air from the french window flow over her. She was cautiously happy that a faint sensation had started in Mike's leg, but she wondered why she should feel mentally worn. It wasn't Mike; his occasional possessive remarks never did make much impression because she allowed for them. Perhaps it was this vivid country of white minarets and brilliant blue skies, of spiky green palms and intensely bright flowers.

When Lucette breezed in about an hour later, it was dusk and Sally was already dressed in tan silk. She looked up from carefully varnishing her nails a petal pink.

"Had a good time?"

"The best!" Lucette spun her straw hat across the room. "I do love it here, Sally. If only you'd come here a year ago, and I'd come to be with you, just as I have now!"

"Why a year ago?"

Lucette pouted her full red lips. "This last year seems to have spoiled so many things." Her mood changed swiftly. "Never mind. I'm loving it. I'd like to stay here for ever!"

"Then you'd better marry a Shiranian."

Lucette walked into the bedroom, and eventually answered with a loud theatrical sigh, "There aren't so many eligible men, you know. Here in the hotel there are just tourists and business-men. Dane is way above all of them."

"And he's not the marrying kind," Sally felt bound to remind her. "He told me so himself."

"Oh, rats to that," called Lucette. "If the Vaugard creature thinks she can get him, why shouldn't someone else have a shot? I think she looks her age."

"Perhaps that's what Dane likes about her. You must admit she's a beauty."

"The hair colour is synthetic!"

"But it's attractive. Stop being feline."

"I've stopped. Guess what? This evening I've a date with a French captain who has a cute moustache!"

"That's a pity. Mike's coming here for dinner; it's the first time since his accident. I wanted you two to meet."

Lucette, stripped almost to the skin, came to the bedroom door. "I'm sorry, but it may be as well if I don't get to know your Mike. I've always had a horror of . . . of illness and cripples."

Sally's smile vanished. She said abruptly, "Don't you dare let Mike know that. Don't you dare!"

Lucette's thin black brows arched, incredulously. "You look like a tigress protecting her cub. I won't let him know, of course. Good lord, Sally, I'm not such a horror as that."

Sally looked down at her fingers and blew upon the drying varnish. "I just don't want anything to impede Mike's recovery, that's all. Hurry up in the bathroom. We may as well go down together."

They couldn't have looked more different from each other as they descended to the vestibule. Sally was slim, her tan silk skirt billowed, and her bronze head was shot with fire under the lights. Lucette sparkled in a narrow dress of emerald brocade; diamonds studded her ear-lobes and collared her neck, and an emerald butterfly had settled inextricably in her hair. She glowed at everyone she met, went happily out on to the terrace and sat down at a table with Sally.

Mike arrived in the hotel car, and Sally willed herself to remain seated while the driver allowed his shoulder to take Mike's weight. As he came up the shallow steps on to the veranda she stood up, smiling. He was breathless and pale, but her calmness about seating him drew an answering smile from him.

"Well, you made it," she said. "And now you must meet Lucette. Mike Ritchie . . . Lucette Millar."

Mike sat back, looked at Lucette rather hard. He echoed her surname. "Sally says you come from Tangier. Are you Tom Millar's daughter?"

Lucette blinked twice, rapidly. "Yes. Yes, I am. You . . . don't know my father, by any chance?"

"No, only that he's a director of the Midi Press. I used to do an article for them every week."

Lucette seemed to have lost her usual volubility. "But you're out of touch with them now?"

He nodded down at his leg. "Probably for good."

Too obviously, Lucette gave a relieved sigh. She quickly looked away from the leg and said stiltedly, "Sally's hoping for great things. I hope it won't take too long."

"So do I," said Mike. "Shall we order drinks?"

But just then Lucette's French captain, complete with his cute moustache, clicked his heels and bowed at her side. She made a hurried introduction, slipped a confiding arm into the crook of his elbow and tripped away with him.

Mike stared after her. "You're right, Sally. She's some girl."

"I'm afraid she'd already made the date when I got back this afternoon."

"That's all right. She likes her men whole and handsome."

"Now, Mike!" Sally looked round quickly for a waiter. "What will you have?"

They ordered, and Sally wished to heaven she hadn't come down with Lucette. She tried several topics and got nowhere, she hoped for Tony, but there was no sign of him.

Mike seemed to guess at her thoughts, for he said, "Tony's out tonight. There's a bachelor party at Le Perroquet."

"Oh. Does Cécile Vaugard sing at that kind of binge?"

"No, she's upstage about them. They've probably put the party on purposely, while she's away."

"Is she away? I haven't seen her about, but then I never do; she keeps to her rooms. I thought she was engaged to sing at Le Perroquet for some weeks yet."

"So she is, but she took a week off. I don't suppose she's really important at the phosphate mine, but she always insists on being included in all the discussions."

Sally's fingers curled tightly round her glass. "Do you mean she's gone with Dane?"

"Would she miss a chance like that? The phosphate mine is miles from anywhere. They'll both stay with the manager and his wife, and business will be generously mixed with pleasure." As if he hadn't said enough, Mike tacked on, "You see, they can't really enjoy one another here at the Mirador, because she's well known and Dane belongs here. Out at the mine they can be themselves."

Sally nodded, and said nothing. She kept a smile for Mike, but inside she felt forlorn and depleted, and there was a cold little block where her heart should be.

CHAPTER SIX

Two days later, Lucette celebrated her twenty-second birth-day. Somehow she contrived that the hotel arrange the day for her, while she basked in good wishes from the many guests with whom she had made friends, and gifts from people Sally had never heard of. Suite Seven filled with flowers and caskets of chocolates and perfumes, and at lunch-time the orchestra played a spectacular version of "Happy Birthday to You." Lucette received homage as if she were a naughty princess, and issued a general invitation for dancing and a special buffet from ten o'clock onwards.

Miraculously, a gigantic birthday cake appeared that night in the entrance to the transformed dining-room. When Lucette exclaimed her rapture, Pierre de Chalain explained that it was Dane's gift in his absence.

Lucette sparkled at Sally. "There! I told Dane the date of my birthday only once, and he remembered it! He actually left instructions for the cake to be prepared for today. And you say he hasn't a soul above business!"

Pierre smiled. "Perhaps you two mademoiselles each see a different Dane. To you, Mademoiselle Lucette, he is a man and not an employer. Our good Miss Yorke would not wish to appeal to his senses."

Sally lifted her shoulders in reply to the rather challenging statement; her gesture was part of the bright shell she was growing. She said conventionally, "You've had the room beautifully decorated, monsieur. I always wonder where the tables and carpets disappear to on these occasions."

He answered charmingly, "That is a little of the art of hotel-keeping, mademoiselle. We have our secrets." The orchestra began to play and he beamed upon the performers before turning back to Sally. "You will permit me the pleasure of the first dance?"

"I'd be delighted."

He danced well, was as light and experienced on his feet as his son. He asked about Mike, and said that with luck the young man would be able to attend the next function which came along. Then Pierre glanced sideways at the jewelled bracelet Sally wore.

"It is an elegant trinket, mademoiselle. It was a twenty-first birthday gift, no doubt?"

"No, I'm afraid it wasn't. Lucette insisted that I should wear it tonight. It's hers."

"So? Your friend is amazingly generous with her possessions. Her family are very rich?"

"No, they're not. The bracelet was among some oddments left to Lucette by her grandmother. It's all imitation stuff."

Pierre looked at her searchingly, glanced again at the mixture of sapphires and diamonds about her wrist. "Those are not fake gems, mademoiselle," he said quietly. "The bracelet you wear is worth at least three thousand pounds."

Sally stopped dancing abruptly, and brought up her arm to inspect the glittering ornament. Almost with horror she said, "Are you sure, monsieur? If you are, I can't possibly wear it."

Pierre examined it more closely. "It seems to have a good safety catch – one of the most modern. I would say there is no risk of losing it."

"But I'm not taking the chance. Will you put it in your safe for me? I'm sure Lucette doesn't realize how much the thing is worth!"

Pierre accepted the bracelet and smiled. "I would say Mademoiselle Lucette has a good idea of the value of the bracelet. She herself is wearing one as costly, and two fine rings." He gave his deep shrug. "She has expensive tastes, that one, and it seems natural that she should own good jewellery." He bowed. "If you will excuse me, I will lock this up at once."

Sally nodded, and began drifting towards the long buffet tables to inspect the canapés and wines and flowers. But she was thinking of Lucette's jewellery, several items of which still

97

lay upstairs in the dressing-table drawer. True, the drawer was locked, but it was appalling to think of the fantastic value of its contents. Staring, unseeing, at a dish heaped with oyster patties, Sally found herself wondering about Lucette. Several months ago she had written that she owned almost nothing, but she had appeared at the Mirador loaded with luxurious clothes, jewels and enough ready cash to buy a villa, if she'd wanted one. And Pierre was right; Lucette was clever enough to know genuine jewels when she saw them. She had pretended the stuff was synthetic to hoodwink Sally. But why?

Sally looked down at the soft blue dress she wore. It was simply cut and unspectacular, and she had been willing to remain as anonymous as it made her feel. But Lucette, buoyant and glossy in dark red and diamonds, had sighed and shaken her head.

"My little bracelet is the touch you need. There are earrings to match it. *Please*, Sally."

Sally had refused, but in the end consented to wear only the bracelet. She had actually been stupid enough to say, "The stones look real, Lucette. I didn't know artificial gems could be so good."

To which Lucette had replied airily, "My grandmother had good taste. If her jewellery had to be phoney, it must be the very best phoney. It suits you, darling – takes away that clinical look you seem to carry about with you even out of uniform."

And Sally had been disarmed.

Now she looked for Lucette, and saw her dancing with the French captain who had made a hit with his moustache. Sally watched, and felt a qualm. Lucette had changed from the flirtatious girl of the past into a slightly dangerous woman. And her habit of lying, apparently, had been converted into a defensive weapon of large dimensions. In schooldays she had been lovable in spite of her faults. Now she was gay and magnetic, but her most endearing quality, the kitten softness, was assumed only when she felt the need of it. Just a little, Sally was worried.

She danced with Tony, heard his plans for the repairs to the house at the date plantation, consented to help in modernizing the kitchen. A little later, when they were having drinks on the terrace, Tony was oddly quiet. He leaned close to the terrace wall and regarded Sally across the table, but seemed to have no inclination for conversation.

At last, though, he said casually, "I believe I have you to thank for the plantation, Sally. My father's sure of it. If I asked you to become engaged to me and promise to marry me in two years, what would you say?"

Sally looked across the courtyard at the palms and the dark moving sea. "I'd say you're in no position to propose."

"Perhaps not, but that's what I'm doing."

She turned her head towards him sharply. "But, Tony, why? We like each other, but we know we're not in love."

He sounded a little dogged as he answered, "I could love you."

"Could? Sounds a bit hollow. Don't spoil things, Tony."

"I didn't expect you to accept, but you needn't be so unmoved about it." His voice lowered and he picked up a cocktail stick and traced patterns on the table. "Being responsible to Dane is going to be nerve-wearing. I'll need someone strong and comforting. I'm a complete coward sometimes."

"You'll be all right once the business part of it is through and you're living at the plantation. While I'm here I'll back you up." She smiled. "You don't have to offer me marriage to be sure I'll co-operate."

"You'd make a sweet wife," he said regretfully, "and the old chap knows what he's about when he says that marriage stabilizes a man. Dane argued that if you can't work without a wife to fall back upon, you're a poor type. Actually, I don't need a wife just now so much as someone I can talk to at weekends. I know that sounds horribly selfish . . ."

"It's very sensible. I'll be here at the weekends, Tony."

"For how long?"

"Until Mike doesn't need me any more."

There was a brief silence. Then Tony asked, "Do you think Mike will recover without hospital treatment?"

"It's difficult to say. Will-power goes a long way, but he hasn't much where his leg is concerned. There's a splendid rehabilitation centre in England, but Mike has a horror of going among other cripples, even for a short time."

"I thought he might come here tonight."

Sally shook her head. "He can't bear Lucette."

"Good heavens," said Tony, "she's just the kind he used to fall for. That girl he was crazy about when he had the smash was of the Lucette type. He always said the black-haired beauty slipped under his skin without knowing it."

"Possibly that's one of the reasons he dislikes Lucette. He just doesn't want to be reminded of the old days." Sally smiled. "You don't seem to make any headway with her, Tony."

He put on his lady-killing look, leered engagingly. "I haven't really tried – too much on my mind. In any case, I couldn't live up to those baubles and silks she wears. And on the whole I'd say she's a bit of an empty-brain, your Lucette. Care to take a walk?"

Sally stood up and strolled with him down into the courtyard. Cars were packed in methodically on both sides, and it was necessary to walk in the centre of the drive along to the esplanade. It was one of those cool nights which invariably happen after a hot day in North Africa. The stars stood out from a smooth indigo sky, the palms were majestically still and the sea murmured over the pale sand as if loath to disturb Shiran's serenity. An occasional white-robed figure passed along the road, and as Sally and Tony came to the pillars at the end of the driveway they became conscious of a distant fluting.

Sally was about to comment upon it when a car sped round from the esplanade. Perhaps it was instinct that flung Tony's arm about her as they stood in the blinding beams for a moment; she felt herself pulled back so that the car could pass, was aware that it had braked as if to stop, before it purred slowly round to the foot of the hotel steps.

"Dane," said Tony under his breath. "He was due to return tomorrow."

Sally's throat went tight. "Was that Cécile with him?"

"Yes. We're back on the merry-go-round. Oh well, the peace was good while it lasted. Shall we go back?"

He took Sally's arm and led her away and back towards the hotel. They passed under an arch that was faceted with mosaics, crossed a short public garden and came to one of the side gates to the Mirador grounds.

"That was pleasant," said Sally, as they went towards the terrace. "I don't suppose Lucette has missed us, but we ought to go in. Will you go out to the lagoon with Mike and me tomorrow?"

"I'll try. If I can't make it, I'll let you know."

They were at the terrace doors into the dining-room, blinking a little at the brilliance of the lights. The crowd were eating and dancing, laughing, chattering and drinking a great deal. And Lucette was in the centre of them.

Behind Sally, Dane said, "Your father wants you, Tony. You can leave Sally with me."

She turned swiftly and looked up. Her heart thudded and sent blood to her cheeks, but caution kept the excited greeting from passing her lips. Instead she said evenly, "Hallo, Dane. Had a good trip?"

"So-so," he said coolly. "Like a drink?"

"A small one, please."

He called a waiter, told him to bring the drinks to the terrace, then moved and indicated she was to go first. For some reason he had no intention of touching her. She smiled at Tony as he left them, but within a second felt her smile fade. She felt shivery, yet her heart still beat too quickly while her pulses told her that this was Dane, who had been away for what seemed like a year.

"Sit down," he said abruptly, when they reached a screened table. "Are you warm enough?"

"Yes, thank you." She paused. "Are you in a bad mood?"

"I wasn't, till I got here."

"Has something upset you?"

"Upset isn't quite the word."

Just then he said no more, for the waiter appeared with whisky, gin and fruit drinks. Dane poured something for Sally, gave himself whisky and water, added ice and sat back. Without the usual salute, he took down half his drink and set the glass back on the table. His face was dark and unreadable, but Sally could see the jut of his jaw and pinpoints of light in his eyes. She found herself wishing they were seated among the illuminations, but she hadn't quite the courage to ask him to switch on more terrace lights. So she sipped, and listened to the noise of Lucette's party.

At last Dane said, "Haven't wasted any time, have you? Had you been necking when I nearly knocked you down on the drive?"

"Necking?" she echoed, outraged. "We were taking a walk!"

"In the middle of a party?"

"It's an impromptu affair – nothing formal. It's most unfair of you to make such an accusation."

He shrugged, sourly. "Looked to me as if you were coming from a car and still in a clinch."

"We weren't, but don't apologize!"

"I'm not going to." He got out cigarettes and shook one free so that she could take it, helped himself and found his lighter. "What else have you been doing while I've been away?"

"Else! You seem to have acquired a poisonous frame of mind. I've been earning my salary and taking a spot of pleasure during my free hours. Do you want a report on Mike's progress?"

He lit her cigarette. "If you like."

She puffed quickly at the cigarette, then held it and lay back. "I've been exercising him each morning, swimming with him in the afternoon and massaging the leg each evening. I did it a little earlier tonight because of the party."

"Any response?"

"He's getting about, but one day soon he'll come to a full

stop. He needs deeper therapy than I can give him here – baths and so on. He's swimming very well."

"Do you two go alone?"

"No, we still take Tony, or meet him at the lagoon. I could manage Mike alone, but if he did get cramp in his right leg and I had to tow him in, he'd be humiliated and hate me afterwards. That wouldn't do him any good."

"Besides," Dane said deliberately, "it must be pleasant to have Tony along. Makes you feel like a woman as well as a nurse."

Sally stubbed out the newly-lit cigarette on the ashtray. "You're impossible. I've no designs on Tony, and you know it."

"All right, forget it. What about getting Mike to go to England for treatment – no progress?"

"None, so far. I wish I knew why he won't leave Morocco."

"You could have known, if you'd asked. Mike's flame at the time of the accident hurried her parents back to England. From something he let drop while he was in hospital, I gathered that he'd do anything rather than meet her again. He has a morbid conviction that if he leaves Morocco he'll run into her."

"But that's silly. The chances are all against it."

"He knows that, but he has time to brood." Dane inhaled and blew smoke. "How do you feel about Mike, as a person?"

"At the moment his personality is too coloured by his . . . lameness to be really pleasant, but when he forgets himself he's a dear." She looked away, towards the sea. "There's been a sort of complication. One day he felt so good that he decided to come here for dinner. I thought it an excellent opportunity to have him meet Lucette, but it was a fiasco. Lucette tried not to show that she's uneasy with anyone infirm or crippled, but Mike's sensitive enough to feel it. He wouldn't come here again."

Dane lifted his shoulders. "It had to happen some time. You can't blame Lucette."

She wanted to look at him, but wouldn't. "No, it wasn't her fault. She's so pretty and full of life that I thought she could help him. I wouldn't have arranged the meeting other-wise."

"You're a good nurse, Miss Yorke. You have the right slant."

"Is that sarcasm?"

"No, but if I were you I'd leave things alone for a bit." His tone changed. "It seems that Lucette is doing very well for herself right here in the hotel. I think she must be after a millionaire."

"I'm sure her little affairs are harmless."

"So am I. In fact, I rather like your friend."

Sally drew in her lip. Off-handedly she asked, "Did you get through your business at the phosphate mine?"

"Pretty well. We appointed an assistant manager. For three solid days we interviewed applicants – two hours each."

"And for the rest of the week?" she queried casually.

"For the rest of the week, young Sally, we looked into other things and paid a few overdue social calls." He added mock-ingly, "Did you miss me?"

A tide of alarm rose in Sally, but she smiled. "Yes, I did, rather. When you're about I'm on guard all the time. I don't know why it is."

"Don't you?" with the same mocking inflection. "I think I know why it is. You wish Mike or someone else were your employer, so that you could be your normal self with me. But you don't do too badly, my child. I'll bet few other employees have ever talked to an employer as you have to me, and got away with it."

"On the other hand," she pointed out, "you must be the most exacting employer in the world, and you're not exactly indulgent towards me, either."

"I'm just a man."

To Sally, this was the understatement of the year. "You suspect almost everything I do," she accused him.

"That's because you look so sweet," he said cynically. "You're not very tall, but you have a long slim look, like a girl posing as a woman. You wear a steel wristwatch . . ."

"A very good watch! My father gave it to me when I got my diploma."

"Don't get heated; I'm sure your father is a great chap. But we're talking about the over-all effect on you. That's a pretty dress you're wearing, but it needs something to lift it out of the ordinary. With that bronze hair you could be quite striking."

"I don't want to be striking."

"Yet I'll bet," he said coolly and reflectively, "that Cumbria is losing its pull. Shake it off, little one, and take a good look at yourself next time you use a lipstick."

"Aren't you afraid," she said in tones which had gone a little hard, "that if I make myself more attractive Tony will neglect his plantation? It could happen, you know."

"I don't think so," he answered easily. "You see, I had a word with Pierre as soon as I got in this evening. Tony leaves tomorrow, and he's to report here only once a month."

Sally sat there, disliking him intensely. "You did it because you saw us on the drive, didn't you? Well, I think your way of dealing with Tony is beastly, and there'll be nothing to stop him coming to Shiran if he wants to. He doesn't have to stay at the Mirador. He could visit Mike . . ."

He leaned forward suddenly, jammed his cigarette into the ashtray and said curtly, "Mike won't invite him – I'll see to that. Too bad you have to lose your most ardent admirer, but you'll get used to it."

"What I feel about it isn't important," she returned at once. "Tony hasn't been accustomed to solitude and it's hateful of you to thrust him into a position that he can't alter. Occasionally, he'll want to talk things over with his father . . ."

"There'll be nothing to stop Pierre visiting him!"

"He'll need a change from everlasting date palms. He's been used to a little fun now and then, and plenty of companionship. Anyone of his type would go nuts if they were cut off from everything."

"He won't collapse during the first month," Dane said grimly. "We'll wait and watch."

"You're being vindictive."

"I'm not. Tony has to prove himself, and he'll never do it while he can go to his father when he wishes or drape himself round a woman. There are lots of tougher assignments than the one he's taking on. Your kind of softness is bad for a fellow like Tony, and the sooner you realize it the better it'll be for both of you."

Sally was breathing as if she'd walked a hard mile. She stood up and found him standing with her. "I think I know what's in your mind. You want me to hurry up and persuade Mike to take hospital treatment, so that you can send me away. I'm bad for Tony, because I'm willing to understand him. But you don't want him understood. You want him to force himself into a precision-type plantation manager, because any project you take up has to succeed! Nothing at all must stand in the way of that, and it mustn't take too long either. As soon as anyone becomes an associate of yours he has to cut out the human element and become a machine . . ."

"That's enough! I'm acting as I think best for Tony . . . and for you."

"For me!" she flung at him. "All you've ever done for me is to establish me in a luxury I didn't want and pay me a large salary. Even your kindness springs from some feeling of superiority. I'm just someone you generously brought out from England for Mike . . . and now you've decided I'm not working on him quickly enough. All right, Mr. Ryland, get someone else! I'm through."

He grabbed her shoulders before she could move. "You little idiot," he said through his teeth. "How the hell did we arrive at this? I'm not dissatisfied with the way you're working on Mike – far from it. If you hadn't let yourself go a little crazy over Tony everything would be just right."

Sally was trembling. "Does interest in Tony mean that I'm crazy over him? Won't you believe that it's sometimes possible for a woman to see deeper than you can?" The fire went out of her. "It's no good. I've known for some time that I'll never be really happy here, and that I'll never be able to satisfy you completely. For Mike's sake, it's best that I leave soon. Anyone with a knowledge of massage could do what I'm doing for him, and I'd be willing to . . . to train someone . . ."

The whole scene had become too much for Sally. She wasn't weeping, but her throat seemed clogged with salt and she felt hollow and weary. She knew that Dane was angry, far more angry than she had ever seen him before, but she realized also that there was something which restrained him in that moment. He let go of her shoulders, let out a furious breath.

"For the present," he said, "you're going on as usual with Mike. Tomorrow we'll have a talk, a proper talk."

"More discussion won't do any good. I'd rather go."

"You're staying," he said grimly.

"Am I another of your ventures? Is that why you're determined that I shall stay and succeed with Mike in the least possible time?"

He blazed. "Be careful, young Sally . . ."

And then Cécile came along the terrace, a tall graceful figure in a dark silk suit. In the half-light she rested a glance on Sally's flushed and distressed face, shifted it to the arrogant lean features of Dane Ryland. What she guessed must have pleased her, for she smiled.

"Good evening, Miss Yorke," she said graciously. And to Dane: "*Chéri*, I have word from Le Perroquet that they have a party who wish me to sing for them tonight. I know it is rather late – but as they were good enough to release me for a week, I feel I should oblige them. Will you take me, Dane?"

"Yes, of course," he said automatically. "Are you ready now?"

Cécile laughed musically. "Are you suddenly blind, *mon vieux*? I am wearing the suit in which I travelled. Give me ten minutes to change into an evening gown. I will meet you at the entrance.

"I'll be there."

Cécile turned to Sally. "Shall we walk to the lift together? I would like to know how is this business you have with Mike."

Sally didn't look at Dane. She nodded to Cécile and walked

107

away with her, along the terrace and into the lounge.

Cécile was saying, "Is it possible that Dane reprimanded you out there, mademoiselle? You looked very much like a girl who has lost one of her dearest dreams."

"There was no reprimand," said Sally.

"Well, never mind. If you are here long enough you will learn that Dane has true feeling for only a few people." A pause. Then, pointedly, "You may forget anything I have said to you before about him. Do your work with Mike. He needs you."

This, from Cécile, was bewildering. Later, Sally was to reflect that the woman had merely spoken her thoughts and convictions, that she now saw no danger in Sally Yorke and could treat her as she treated everyone else, with pleasant hauteur. But just then there was a diversion.

Dane had followed them into the hotel by way of the main entrance, and as they waited for one of the lifts, both women saw him speak to Pierre de Chalain, near the reception desk. There came a flurry of dark red topped with dark curls, Lucette's excited exclamation.

"Dane! I didn't know you were back. Did you remember it was my birthday – is that why you came?"

"Could be," Dane said lazily, as he looked at her bright cheeks and sparkling eyes. "How does it feel to be twenty-two?"

"Marvellous!" Lucette closed her eyes and swayed, opened them very wide at him. "Your coming back tonight has really *made* my birthday, do you know that? Oh, and Dane . . . that stupendous cake! It's like the Taj Mahal."

He laughed. "I hope it's more yielding. Have you cut it yet?"

"No, we'll cut it together, as you do a wedding cake." Then Lucette did something typical. She rested her hands on his shoulders, raised herself on to her toes and kissed him warmly on the lips. "There! That means thank you."

The lift slid open and Cécile, her head high and rigid, walked into it. Sally lingered long enough to catch Dane's glance across the vestibule and to become aware of the hint of malice in the smile he gave her. She heard him say teasingly, "You could get away with anything, Lucette, and you certainly know the right length for a first kiss. Come on, I've just time for one dance before I have to go out. I'm sure you're a magnificent dancer."

The lift door closed softly, the small compartment ascended without sound and glided to a halt. Cécile and Sally came out on to the thickly-carpeted hallway, turned along the corridor. Cécile's suite was the most remote from the lift, so they reached Suite Seven together.

Cécile slowed, and asked, "How long does your friend stay at the Mirador?"

"Indefinitely, I think."

"Dane told me about her. She has no fiancé in Tangier?"

"No."

"You invited her here. You must get rid of her."

"I have no influence over Lucette – none whatever."

"Then I will get rid of her myself," said Cécile with icy calm, and she walked on to the end of the corridor.

In her sitting-room, Sally sank down into a chair and leant her head against its back. The smell of the numerous bouquets was so overpowering that it made her aware of her own worn nerves. For some time her mind was almost blank. But presently her thoughts went back over the last hour or so. Had Dane returned because of Lucette? According to Tony, he had been expected back tomorrow, and no doubt Cécile would have been willing to extend their break from routine for another day. But Dane had preferred to return a day earlier, even though the hour of their arrival must be very late.

Yet somehow Sally could not see Dane altering his plans for the volatile young woman he had known only a day or two. He had spoken as if Lucette amused him . . . but he had also defended her attitude to Mike's crippled state; he had condoned in Lucette an antipathy towards illness which Sally regarded as appallingly unfeminine.

She couldn't forget the look he had slanted her own way as she was entering the lift. "Lucette knows how to please a man," it had said; "This is how a woman should be – pliant and captivating, not independent and defiant." Well, let him get what he could out of Lucette. Sally didn't care; she mustn't. There were too many other things that puzzled and hurt her. Dane's cold implacability towards Tony, his determination that she should do what he paid her to do in the way of persuading Mike to enter an orthopaedic hospital – both these made the rest seem comparatively unimportant.

Yet the shock of watching his acceptance of Lucette's kiss returned to her with the impact of a sledge-hammer. As it receded it left her feeling desperate, and lonely as she had never been in her life before; she couldn't understand her own reaction. Surely this wasn't love or need – this gnawing, harrowing sensation which had possession of her?

She snapped on the double lamp between the beds and switched off the main light, padded over to the french window and fastened one of the doors wide open, so that the night air off the sea might find its tortuous way round the hotel and into the room. She looked out and saw that a moon she hadn't noticed before was turning the world pale. There was spice in the air, the smell of exuberant life.

Sally sighed; it was too beautiful to be real. She had been right not to trust the magic of Shiran, but she did wish she *could* have trusted it. She was back in the room and choosing a book from the bedside bookcase when the sitting-room door slammed and Lucette came breezing in. A purse was flung on to a chair, high-heeled slippers were kicked off and Lucette skipped into the bedroom like a child ready for a day's fun. She laughed for the sheer joy of it.

"What a glorious day! And you deserted me, Sally. That wasn't nice."

"It got so late, and I'm a working girl. Besides, you did tell everyone they could fade when they'd had enough."

"So you were bored! That's wicked. I could start all over again, but the crowd have gone to bed." Lucette pushed fingers through her hair, took a delight in making it stand out from her head. "Dane's come back – specially for my birthday. Did you know?"

"Yes, I saw him." Sally caught the glitter of diamonds at the creamy neck and said quickly, "Lucette, that jewellery of yours . . . you must have known it was genuine when you lent me the bracelet this evening."

"Genuine?" Lucette stopped moving, and a veil slipped down over her expressive eyes. "Don't be silly. Would I throw real jewellery about as if it were costume stuff?"

"You might, seeing that you have so much."

"Who told you it's real?"

"Monsieur de Chalain. He said that you must be aware of it, too."

"What did you do with the bracelet?"

"As soon as he told me, I was afraid I'd lose it, so I asked him to lock it up in his safe. And you'll have to put the rest with it. I won't have it left here in the bedroom. It's unnerving." Lucette didn't answer at once, and Sally added slowly, "You've changed, Lucette. Where did you get all this stuff?"

Lucette's head lifted and she said petulantly, "I've told you – from my grandmother."

"How long ago?"

"About five months."

"Then if you'd been so tired of your parents' control, you could have left them weeks ago."

Lucette turned impulsively, made her eyes melting and dark as she smiled with infinite ruefulness at Sally. "You don't understand, petsie, and I can't go into a long-winded explanation at this hour. I admit the jewels are real, and I promise to have them put in the hotel safe tomorrow morning. Will that do?"

Sally turned to her bed. "If you won't tell me more, it will have to do, won't it? I'm sleepy."

"I'm not!" Lucette hugged herself and shifted slightly, so that from her position at the foot of Sally's bed she could see the moon-washed sky and feel the air about her. "You know, darling, I think I'm happier than at any time in my life. I'm in love!"

Sally's fingers curled tightly over the sheet-edge, but she managed to ask lightly, "Are you? With Dane?"

"Who else?" Lucette's voice was vibrant with an exciting emotion. "Just before he went away I felt that magnetism of his and told myself it was only natural that, as I'd been shut up with my parents so long, I'd be terribly aware of the first man who paid me compliments. While Dane was gone, I played with the others, just to find out whether what I felt for Dane was real or a sudden infatuation. I only had to see him again tonight to be sure that it certainly wasn't temporary. I adore the man!"

Sally slid nervously into her bed and lay back. Her lips felt icy and a prickly sensation ran along her spine. "Cécile Vaugard is fond of him, too."

Lucette wrinkled her nose, contemptuously. "She's a beauty, I grant you, but she's waited a little too long. I only hope . . ."

"What?"

"Oh, nothing." She scintillated suddenly. "I'm not going to think back or into the future. Dane finds me attractive and amusing, and I . . . well, I find him devastating. I decided on my way upstairs that I'm going to stay in Shiran till he tells me he loves me. And do you know something, Sally? I'm going to ward off the moment, just to string out the happiness!"

Sally could find no reply to this, and after a moment or two of ecstatic inward contemplation, Lucette trailed off to the bathroom. All desire for sleep had left Sally. She lay with her eyes closed and her mind wide awake, her heart beating unevenly into the bed.

Was Lucette's love for Dane real and lasting? Was Dane finding himself drawn towards the mercurial young woman who could offer him both youth and maturity, as well as a brand of beauty and an effervescent kind of love? Sally didn't know, but she remembered, bleakly, that she herself had brought Lucette to Shiran.

Minutes later, she also remembered Cécile Vaugard's parting words: "Then I will get rid of her myself." And she felt she would have to get up and walk about, or the turmoil inside her would rip her apart. But Lucette came back into the bedroom, humming a little French tune, and slowly Sally recovered and put her emotions back where they belonged. The only way to handle this thing was to look at it coldly, dispassionately and analytically. And she wouldn't be in any condition to do that before the morning.

CHAPTER SEVEN

MIKE, next morning, was morose and quiet. He followed Sally's directions, held on to the bar they had screwed into the veranda wall and obediently swung his leg and bent from the waist, used the steel expander and did a modified form of Swedish drill to keep his shoulder muscles fit. When the session was over, he put the conventional query.

"Like an iced drink?"

Sally shook her head. "Not this morning, Mike. I'll come along as usual this afternoon."

He relaxed in his chair. "Good. I'll be ready."

"Shall I find you a book?"

He hesitated. "No, but you might get me some writing paper and a couple of envelopes from the desk. I want to send off a couple of letters."

"Shall I wait and post them for you?"

"No, that's all right," he said quickly. "Yussef will take them."

She went into the lounge for paper and envelopes, stopped at a side table to pick up her purse and noticed a glove which had been folded small and slipped between the flower vase and a cigarette box. It was an ice-blue glove . . . Cécile's colour.

She went out and fixed Mike up with a table and everything else he needed, said goodbye and got into the car. But as she left the villa she was thinking about Cécile, and her connection with Mike. He wasn't particularly fond of women, Sally was sure, and Cécile's interest in him had always seemed to be prompted by a wish to please Dane. It was possible, of course, that they did have a little in common, but Sally was certain that neither roused emotion in the other.

Had Cécile been to the villa this morning, or had she forgotten the glove on an earlier occasion? Sally thought it had been left this morning and half hidden by Mike; otherwise she would have noticed it before. Yet it was still early, in fact exceptionally early for Cécile to be abroad. Oh well, whatever the reason for Cécile's visit to Mike, it didn't concern Sally Yorke. So after a while Sally forgot it.

At lunch-time Lucette was missing, and upon remarking to the head waiter that the dining-room seemed almost empty, Sally learned that a convoy of hired cars had taken a large number of residents to visit the Saadian Tombs and other sights at Marrakesh; they would return late this evening.

Sally ate crayfish salad and a small fruit mould topped with cream and nuts, took coffee in the nearly deserted lounge and went out to the terrace to wait till the car should come round for her, at three o'clock. She put on sun glasses and looked over the courtyard, wishing, a little forlornly, that she could have been on holiday just for today. Marrakesh was set in desert sands and against a background of jagged mountains. It was full of Spanish-Moslem art and architecture, soaked with history, both violent and cultural. The one city in Morocco, so it was said, that no one should miss. She, Sally, was missing all of Morocco except Shiran.

A car backed from its parking place and slid round the court-yard to the foot of the steps. It was the big silver and blue thing, and Dane got from behind the wheel and came up into the terrace. He looked long and lithe in beige slacks and a matching silk shirt.

Sally tightened, was glad to be wearing dark glasses. She acknowledged his greeting, felt him sink down into the chair at her side.

"It's hot at midday," he said. "You should rest upstairs after lunch."

"It's bearable here. Our suite is so full of flowers that the scent is overpowering."

"Well, have them thrown out. Are you bored?"

"No."

"Still cross with me?"

"I wasn't cross – I was furious."

"That's not very wise. I suppose you'll be more furious when I tell you that Tony's gone. He left while you were with

115

Mike this morning – asked me to say goodbye to you."

"I suppose you wouldn't let him wait to see me?" she asked coolly.

He shrugged. "I wasn't sure how long you'd stay with Mike. You might even have lunched there."

"He could have driven that way and said goodbye to both of us."

"Not very easily. I took him to the plantation myself."

She was silent.

Dane leaned forward and looked along the terrace. "The guests have run out on us in numbers today. It's quite peaceful here. Or are you less peaceful now that I've happened along?"

"How did you guess?"

His smile was sharp. "I said I'd have a talk with you today, but I've decided against it. You need to simmer down a little." A pause. "What were you thinking about while you were alone?"

"About Morocco."

"Really? That's a concession, from you. Not beginning to ache for a spot of tourism, are you?"

"I wouldn't have minded going along with the crowd to Marrakesh today," she admitted offhandedly.

"I'll take you myself, tomorrow."

"No!" She qualified the swift negative: "I don't want to miss a day with Mike, now that we've begun. Perhaps before I leave Morocco I'll make a quick tour of the country."

He sat back. "You do have a time with yourself, don't you? With Tony gone, I knew you'd be touchy today, but I thought you'd mask it a bit. Normally you're pretty good at the stiff upper lip business, but the fact that you won't see him for a month has got you rattled." He sounded crisp and cynical as he added, "You'll get over a kiss or two, little one. I shouldn't think Tony's lovemaking is particularly shattering."

Sally did not rise to the bait. She merely said, with a shrug. "I must call for the car and get my swimsuit. Will you excuse me?"

"While you get bathing gear – yes. As a matter of fact, as

116

Tony's missing, I'll go with you and Mike today. I'll wait right here for you."

She paused and looked at him, saw a tight mocking smile on his lips and a watchfulness in the sea-green eyes. Then she turned away and went into the hotel, and up to her suite. Without thinking, she collected a rose-pink swimsuit and a rubber cap, rolled both inside one of the soft bath towels, and picked up the gay straw bag which held cosmetics and other necessities. Then, as she was leaving the bedroom, her glance rested on the white icing ornament which had decorated the top of Lucette's birthday cake, and something inside Sally hardened and went cold.

She went into the bedroom and took off her dress, slipped on white linen shorts and a tangerine cotton blouse bought at the hotel emporium. She changed from ordinary white sandals into many-coloured straw flatties, gathered up her goods, and without a glance at herself, went out and down the great staircase. As she reached the terrace she put on the sun-glasses; they were the best disguise she knew.

Dane stood up, his brow lifted. His glance went all over her in one swift summing up, he looked for a second time at the graceful lines of her long brown legs and thoughtfully scratched his chin.

"So this is what you've been up to while I was away," he commented. "Maybe I returned only just in time."

Sally did not tell him that this was her first effort at wearing hotel-guest attire. She walked at his side to the car, got into it, and waited for him to take his place and set the car moving. She looked at the trees along the esplanade, was aware of heat gushing into the car with the breeze and of the silent bombardment of Dane's watchfulness. No other man, surely, could contrive to watch his companion closely and drive fast at the same time?

When they reached Mike's house neither had spoken. Mike was in the lounge, and somehow Sally managed to keep a couple of paces ahead of Dane, so that Mike's surprise, if any, should be blunted before he spoke.

His mood, fortunately, had improved since this morning. He was almost expansive.

"Glad to see you, Dane," he said. "Like some refreshment before we set out?"

"Let's wait till we get there," Dane answered. "I've some vacuum jugs filled with iced drinks in the back of the car. How are you feeling, Mike?"

"Not too bad at all. It's all due to Sally, of course."

"You've done most of the work yourself," Sally said. "Pick up your sticks and I'll take your towel." As Dane moved forward to give Mike some help, she exclaimed quickly, "No, please! Mike does this alone."

Mike shot Dane a glance that Sally could not interpret; she wondered momentarily whether Dane understood it himself. Then Mike was on his feet, stumping with his sound foot over the tiles and grunting with the exertion of getting himself down to the path. His teeth were clamped tight, but his lips bared them in an angry smile. However, when he was seated in the back of the car with the left leg along the seat and a cushion in the small of his back, he looked more normal.

"Go ahead, driver," he said.

Dane let in the clutch and they moved out on to the road which had become so familiar to Sally. She turned and talked over the back of the seat to Mike.

"Tony's gone – this morning. From now on he's a date planter."

"Good for Tony." Mike's tones were restrained. "What about the house – is it furnished?"

Dane answered. "Only two rooms of it. The whole place is being reconditioned. It'll be ready for proper furniture in about two months."

"Meanwhile old Tony has to camp out in a shambles!"

"It won't hurt him to rough it slightly. The important thing is to get him busy on the plantation itself."

"It would be, to you. It sounds the hell of a way to live."

"It isn't," said Dane calmly, without turning his head. "I've lived in worse conditions and for longer than two months."

"You're not Tony. You're a super-type."

Sally cast a warning glance at Mike, met eyes which smiled but were just faintly bright with spite. There had always been a slight antagonism in Mike against his cousin, but now it had changed into something more positive. Sally couldn't understand it. Through Dane, Mike was feeling better and moving about under his own steam; he had no reason for resentment. Yet in addition to the existent hostility, suddenly the resentment was there; it was almost tangible.

Little more was said before they had taken the rough thorn-confined lane down to the beach and lagoon. With assistance, Mike levered himself out of the car and went to his usual thick patch of trees to discard his clothing. Sally left the men and climbed the rocks to the cave she used, but when she was in her swim-suit she lingered up there, looking over the boulders which stretched out from this headland and curved round to form the lagoon.

She felt empty and worn; at this moment it seemed impossible that she could go on being agreeable on the surface while she was so tense and anguished underneath. She had had no right to fall in love with Dane, but it had happened, without any of the magic that is supposed to attend such adventures of the heart. Now her position was becoming intolerable, and the days, perhaps weeks ahead, loomed like aeons of insufferable waiting for the time when she could leave Morocco . . . and Dane.

A shout broke into her thoughts. The two men were down there near the edge of the lagoon, and Dane was waving, insisting that she join them. She leapt from rock to rock, descended to the sand and loped towards them, pulling on her cap. Mike was being awkward.

"Tony's not as tall as you are, Dane – I was able to use his shoulder easily. I'd better have Sally."

"We'll manage," Dane said. "She's not an Amazon."

"I can do it," Sally told him. "I've done it before."

"Let Mike find a new way of entering the water." Dane crooked his elbow. "There you are – lean on that."

To get the moment over, Sally waded in up to her waist and swam. She looked back and saw that Mike was hopping furiously into the water while Dane kept a grip on him. Tony had been accommodating, a slim young male who did exactly as Mike told him. Dane was used to running everything he touched, and he had the gaunt strength of an eagle; if Mike had been willing, Dane would have picked him up and carried him into the deeper water.

They swam, Sally on her own and Dane close to Mike. Sally was floating, and thinking deeply. Her hands moved like slow fins and occasionally she felt the fingers nipped by a small outraged fish. Then, quite suddenly, she was aware of the tremendous pull of waves seeping back towards the rocks which enclosed the lagoon, and at the same second she heard a warning shout from Dane. The next moment, as she struggled, the pull came again, so much stronger than before that it dragged her swiftly into the rocks. She felt a sickening thud on the right side of her skull, saw the sky tip drunkenly and go black for an agonizing minute before it righted itself.

Then Dane was at her side, hauling at her waist and wresting her back from a third tidal drag. He got her away, his arm like a steel band about her – and even in her stress Sally remembered that other time when his arm had saved her. He thrust her back into the calm water of the lagoon and hauled her into the shallows. From her knees, she got shakily to her feet.

"God, I thought you'd crash into the rocks," he said, and she realized he didn't know. "What made you go that far?"

"I . . . I was floating and didn't notice. Dane, look . . . after Mike."

"You scared the wits out of me," he said roughly. "Don't come in again."

"I'll . . . dress, I think," she managed, and staggered up the beach.

Dane swam back towards Mike, and after a moment in which she was able to pull her cap from her head and get her bearings, Sally trudged slowly towards the rocks. Her vision blurred, her head swam. Somehow she forced herself upwards from rock to rock and reached the cave. She was out of sight now, and able to sink down on to the sandy floor of the cave and hold a head that felt ten times heavier than it should. The pain was unbelievable, yet she had only broken the skin slightly over an area the size of a halfpenny. Odd that the cap hadn't torn.

She forced herself to move, pushed off the swim-suit and pulled on the blouse and shorts; after which she had to rest again and close her eyes. Her whole head was aching now, and it was worst behind the eyes. She thought, bleakly, that massage across the back of her neck and shoulders would have helped, but it was something she couldn't do for herself.

With a tremendous effort, she picked up the wet suit, cap and towel and came out into sunshine that seemed at once to find the sore spot in her scalp. She was half-way down the rocks when Dane reached her, already clad in his slacks and shirt. He put out a hand to steady her, looked keenly at her pale face.

"The remnants of wind-up, or don't you feel well?" he asked quickly.

"I'll be all right. Where's Mike?"

"Dressing. I gave him one of the vacuum jugs, but the other is still intact. Come on, we'll get a drink."

His concern made him companionable. He slipped an arm across her shoulders and half lifted her down on to the beach, kept the arm there as they walked towards the trees where the car stood. He poured ice-cold grenadilla laced with gin, gave her the beaker while he poured another. They drank slowly and in silence. She refused a second drink and he opened the car door.

"Sit in," he said. "I'll get Mike."

Only a few remarks were exchanged on the way back to Shiran. Knowing that Sally was accustomed to the lagoon, Mike apparently thought that Dane had become alarmed over nothing, but he did ask how she felt. When Dane pulled up outside the villa and told Sally to remain in the car, Mike's lip curled.

With heavy sarcasm, he said, "You're able to appropriate the girls now, Dane, and I'm just an onlooker. Times change, don't they?"

"So do tastes, old chap," came the reply. "I'll help you indoors."

Sally waited. Dane came back and started the car, swung it out on to the road. She was not thinking very clearly, but she did wonder how it was that a man whose reactions were often violent could remain calm and even kindly towards someone who was obviously goading himself into hate for him. This afternoon she had seen a facet of Dane that she hadn't quite known existed. She wished she felt equal to analysing it; at the moment she could only reflect that Mike's game leg put him, for Dane, beyond retaliation in any form. But what, more than usual, could be eating Mike? Some of his comments had been rude and malicious, and it had angered him that Dane remained even-tempered and as helpful as ever.

At the Mirador, Dane ran alongside the hotel and pulled up. He came round to her door, kept his hand at her elbow as they crossed the foyer to the lift. Sally was glad of that hand giving its strength. She stood in the lift as they floated upwards, quivered a little as the lift halted and the doors slid open. More than anything she wanted to lie down on her bed.

But Dane did not lead her towards Suite Seven. He guided her to the left, opened the door of his own apartments and gently pushed her inside. She found herself in the room in which she had first seen him; felt the breeze through the open french windows as she had then and saw the couple of landscapes above the desk – which she hadn't noticed that first time.

Dane indicated a brown silk-covered divan. "Relax a bit. I'll get you a proper drink."

Dazedly, she remembered that Cécile had lain there one night, complaining of a bogus laryngitis, and shook her head. The action sent a knife into her scalp and she winced. Dane came close, took her by the shoulders and looked deeply into her face. Then, not quite audibly, he swore.

"You *did* get hurt out there. Was it your head?"

"It smarts a bit – only a graze."

"Why the deuce didn't you tell me?"

"It wasn't much use, and I didn't want Mike to know."

"Damn Mike! He's had so much consideration that he's gone soft and stupid with it. Sit down, for heaven's sake, and let me look at this graze."

She sat as he stood over her, parting the short bronze hair gently with his fingers till he found the small clot of dark blood. He made another sound under his breath, told her to sit still and went into the bathroom. A minute later he was snipping the clotted hair and sponging the wound with an antiseptic solution. He snipped again, and foggily Sally wondered what she would look like when he had finished. She felt an adhesive dressing pressed over the abrasion, the front hair smoothed backwards to hide it.

In odd tones he was saying, "Why did you do it, Sally – go so far across the lagoon? You've been there many times and nothing of this kind has happened, but today, when I'm there, you drift straight into danger. Why?"

"You can't really explain these things," she said in low tones. "Previously I've stayed near Mike because . . . well, Tony is young and sometimes thoughtless, and I wanted to be sure of Mike's safety. Today, of course, it was different. You'd taken over with Mike and I was free to swim or let myself go."

"You could have done it closer to Mike and me."

She looked down at the fingers which were locked together in her lap. "Yes, I know. It was very foolish."

He turned away and poured a small whisky, added a little soda and put the glass into her hand. "Take it right down."

"Ought I to mix my drinks?"

"You're young enough to survive it," with just a hint of mockery. "Besides, the whisky will make you sleep. You're going to bed, young Sally. I'll let Mike know that you're not going there this evening, and if you want to, you can sleep through till the morning."

"I couldn't do it."

"You must rest, anyway." He paused. "I intended to tell you while we were out this afternoon that I've had another letter from the Caid who asked me to bring a party to his kasbah. He wants us there by six tomorrow evening."

"Perhaps I oughtn't to go. Mike . . ."

"You'll take time off from Mike," he said abruptly. "I know you're doing all you possibly can for him, but I'm also pretty sure that you were right when you said that your treatment can only have a limited effect. He's got to go away for the whole works. There's no hurry, but he'll have to go."

"All right," she said wearily, "but don't be dictatorial with him about it. I'd like to go to my room now."

Dane took her there, walked with her into the bedroom. Lucette's bed was strewn with her play-suit, gay scarves which she must have discarded in favour of a particular colour, and one straw slipper. Dane gave the array a tolerant glance and turned to fold back the lavender cover on Sally's bed and transfer it to a stool. Because she was feeling like death but unwilling to let him suspect it, Sally stepped out of her slippers and lay down. He covered her with a sheet and one of the thin cellular blankets, stood looking down at her.

"You're not to worry about a thing. That clear?"

"Yes."

"I'll come in and see you later on."

"No, don't!" She felt a painful drumming in her throat. "I'll sleep. I promise. And . . . and thank you."

"For what?" His tone had a faint edge. "You banged your head because you were getting as far away from me as you could. Some time we'll get to the bottom of it all – but not now. Go to sleep. I'll keep Lucette out of the way; when she gets back from Marrakesh I'll arrange another outing. I did once say I'd show her the old palace, here in Shiran."

Sally said baldly, "Yes, do that – show her the old Moorish palace in the moonlight." Then she turned her head from him and pressed her cheek into the cool pillow.

She thought, prayed, that he would go then. But he didn't. She felt him there behind her, close to the bed. Then, without a warning sound of any sort, he was bending near, his breath warm across her cheek. Briefly, his lips touched her temple. Then he crossed the room and left the suite.

A suffocating pain gripped Sally, a pain which bore no relation to the physical soreness of the little wound. He had bestowed a light kiss, as though she were a hurt child who needed comfort. He had done his best for her in the circumstances, and now he could wade back into the business of living and forget her. That was Dane, whether she could bear it or not.

Sally was up and about next morning, with pale cheeks and a tight heart. But her expression was serene and unrevealing, and she smiled when Lucette grumbled, from the depths of her bed, that it was a sin to rise before nine. She drank some coffee and ate a roll in the sitting-room, went downstairs to discover that mail had been waiting in her pigeon-hole since yesterday afternoon. There was a letter from her mother, and two postcards from children at the Beckmoor. All three brought back the scents of home, but the heat and brilliance of Shiran quickly dispelled them. That was the trouble with Morocco, thought Sally; it robbed every other place of colour and point.

She walked in the grounds, avoiding the pool and the paths nearest the hotel. She trod the mosaics round the fountain and watched the shimmering cascade for a while. She let the peace of clipped trees and shrubs, of trilling birds and the murmur of the sea seep into her till her watch said ten minutes to ten, when she walked back to the courtyard and found the usual hotel car waiting for her.

It was exactly ten o'clock when she walked into Mike's lounge and found him seated at a table, working out a chess problem.

"Don't move," she said, and sat down opposite him.

"Never asked you to play chess with me, have I?" he said. "Care for a game?"

"Yes, some time. Is this a problem you read somewhere?"

He nodded. "It was in a paper from England. Mate the

king in three moves.''

Sally rested an elbow on the table and stared at the pieces. Novice's luck was with her, she made the correct first move and followed it up with the inevitable second and third.

Mike gazed at her. "Good lord," he said soberly. "Did you know what you were doing?"

"No, it just happened. I don't suppose I'll ever do it again in my life."

"For me, once was enough. I've been at this for half an hour." He shoved the pieces into their box and closed the lid. "Do we exercise first, or talk?"

"Talk, if you're in the mood."

"Feel better this morning?"

"Yes, thank you. Sorry I couldn't make it last night. You did get Dane's message, I suppose?"

His mouth turned down at the corners. "Dane came himself, at about eight. He had that friend of yours with him."

"Oh." Sally ignored the sudden dryness of her lips. "Did she come in to see you?"

"I was having dinner on the veranda. She didn't get out of the car, but I received a benign smile and a nod of the head. She didn't have to look away from me, you see – my leg was out of sight."

"Don't be silly, Mike. Lucette's a bit childish in that direction, but you're making too much of it. She hasn't been trained, as I have."

"I'll bet you were never disgusted by a man's lameness even before you trained."

"Well, of course not, because my inclination was to help such people." She traced the squares on the chess board. "I know why you dislike Lucette – she's the kind you used to fall for rather heavily, and you now imagine you're not in the least attractive to any woman."

"It's true."

"I don't believe it, but you'll have to discover things for yourself."

"That's life, isn't it?"

"I'm afraid so." She paused. "Dane was taking Lucette to see the sights by moonlight. Did he tell you that?"

Mike shrugged, disagreeably. "Not he. He didn't explain her being with him at all. Why should he, anyway? Isn't he Dane Ryland, who can have any woman he wants and leave the last one flat?"

She lifted a blue gaze to his face. "What's the matter with you, Mike? Since I've known you, you've always been casual towards Dane, and in a way I thought it understandable. You've had to accept a great deal from him, and he's whole and strong. But suddenly it's not just coolness – you hate him. Why?"

The thin face went a little blank and he turned away his head.

"I don't hate Dane as a man – I never have. I've never even disliked his being successful in business – not really. It's . . . well, you wouldn't understand."

"I might," she said quietly.

There was a silence during which Sally decided he felt he had said enough. Then, surprisingly, he turned back towards her and leaned across the table. The expression in his hazel eyes was dark and brooding.

"Cécile is heartbroken – did you know that?"

Sally's fingers tightened under the edge of the table. "Heartbroken? That isn't a condition I'd ever imagine could be associated with Cécile Vaugard. Does she come to see you often?"

"She's been once or twice. Apart from you, she's the only woman I've been able to speak to since I crocked up. When you first came, she told me you might make a play for Dane. I laughed her out of it and she admitted it was foolish. Then Lucette Millar turned up – and she was an entirely different dish." He drew in his lip, then let it go and added, "Your friend has really gone overboard about Dane. Last night she was twenty feet from me, but it came over like waves of electric current. She's besotted about him."

Sally swallowed, but contrived a smile. "That's Lucette's

way. She'll recover, and anyway, no one's really hurt."

"Except Cécile."

"I can't believe she'd take it seriously. Dane likes Lucette, but he's not in love with her."

"In my opinion he's not in love with Cécile, either."

"You . . . you really think that?"

"I'm pretty sure of it. Dane couldn't love anyone. But Cécile was the woman he meant to marry, till your vivacious comrade appeared. I like Cécile, and I loathed seeing her cry."

"She . . . *cried*?"

He threw out his hands impatiently. "She was upset and she upset me. There's Dane, sitting back and letting the women fall over themselves for his attentions, and Cécile pushed out by a brainless little piece of sex-appeal who hasn't as much feeling in her whole body as Cécile has in her fingertips. Do us all a favour, Sally, and send Lucette back to Tangier!"

"I can't send her back before she's willing to go," Sally said helplessly, "and you're wrong about her. She's not vicious and brainless. She has sudden passions for people and things, but they wear off and no one's the worse. Cécile hasn't the least reason to worry about Lucette's effect on Dane."

"You don't see the whole of it. Cécile's tour has been altered and she has to leave Shiran in about nine days for Casablanca. She's quite desperate to get Lucette out of the way before she leaves."

"If Cécile is so fond of Dane," said Sally warmly, "let her give up the tour and stay."

"But singing is part of her life."

"As much a part as her marriage would be?" Sally asked shortly.

"I don't know. I only know that I like Cécile and detest that curvaceous spoiled creature who can't bear to look facts in the face!"

Sally was silent. She realized how he felt far more plainly than he knew. He was influenced less by Cécile's unhappiness than by his own remembered humiliation at the hands of Lucette. His intensified dislike of Dane had been automatic, because Dane derived a degree of pleasure and amusement out of Lucette.

"Do you think Cécile will do anything drastic?" she asked.

He blinked, and his eyes seemed to go pale and distant. "I don't know," he said offhandedly. "Let's get the exercises over, shall we?"

An hour later, when he was back in his veranda chair and they had drunk mint tea together, Sally got up to leave.

"You're looking better every day, Mike," she said. "The swimming agrees with you and it's making you brown."

"There's not to be any for you this afternoon, so I understand."

"No? Was that Dane's decision?"

"He says you're doing too much and must rest. He's asked a young chap who's staying at the hotel to go with me this afternoon. Big of him, isn't it?"

"You mustn't mind, for a day or two. I did get a bad head yesterday."

"Yes, I know. I'm sorry." He stared at the table, then raised his glance so that it met and held hers. "You know, Sally, I'm coming to the point where I'd go over to England if you'd guarantee to stick with me over there – get a job wherever I might be admitted."

Her heart seemed to drop to the bottom of a cavity. "Are you? Are you really?"

"I'm coming to it," he said cautiously. "I'm not there yet, but I do think about it."

"That's good, Mike." But she felt raw as she spoke. "Have you told anyone else?"

"Hell, no. When I decide I can face it, you'll be the first one to know."

"Fine. Go on thinking that way."

He was about to say more, but Sally had had enough. She touched his shoulder lightly, and said goodbye and went down to the car. She sat behind the driver, and they were gliding down the road towards the esplanade when she began to think over Mike's final piece of news.

The terrible thing had been her own sudden and shattering reaction to it. She was a physiotherapist, engaged for the purpose of persuading an obstinate young man to enter an orthopaedic hospital or rehabilitation centre, yet at the first sign of capitulation she had thought, *"Oh, no, not yet! I can't leave this place . . . not yet!"* She had put her own emotions before professional integrity, had hastily decided that Mike need not be hurried to make his decision. And why? Because the very thought of leaving Dane was a sword at her heart. Here in Shiran she felt insecure and tormented, but at least she was near him. When she left it would be like going into oblivion, or worse.

Lord, what a pass she had come to!

She took a deep breath, bracing herself to meet the Mirador. As the car stopped, Dane came down the steps and leaned forward to open the door. He was smiling, an arrogant watchful smile, and when she stood beside him he said, "You're looking more yourself. How's the bump?"

"Not so bad, if I avoid touching it. You did a good job of trimming the hair. It doesn't show at all."

"Good. Did Mike tell you about my arrangements?"

She nodded. "He'll be all right with a stranger at the lagoon. I'll see him tonight."

"Haven't forgotten we're visiting the Caid, have you?"

"Is it certain? I ought to have told Mike."

"I'll let him know. Have a good rest this afternoon – the evening is likely to be tiring. We'll leave at about five." A pause, and then with a hint of satire, "Like me to put you to bed again? I do it well, don't I?"

But Sally was in no mood for his stringent sort of banter. She answered, "With practice, one can do anything well, Mr. Ryland," and walked into the hotel.

Her every nerve was aware that he had followed her only for a pace or two. Then, too angry to trust himself entirely, he had gone through to the manager's office, to work it off.

Sally went up to Suite Seven, weighed down by an intolerable sense of failure.

CHAPTER EIGHT

THE approach to the kasbah was a green corridor between low blue mountains; a valley filled with fields of corn and mandarin groves, cork-oak forests, and expanses of cedar and juniper. There were a few vineyards, extensive pasturelands covered closely with cattle and sheep, and a river bubbling shallowly over stones and disappearing among the cultivation. The kasbah itself became visible as they rounded a dry craggy mountain: an ornamental stone wall, within which were a collection of closely-built dwellings and the beautifully sculptured residence of the Caid.

Sally leaned forward to obtain her first close look at the true heart of Morocco – a small, self-contained village in mountain country, ruled over by a Moor of education and breeding.

She was sitting in the back of the blue and silver car with Pierre de Chalain. Lucette had the front seat and therefore the best view, which was a pity; her only interest in this evening visit to the kasbah had been the fact that Dane was in charge. To Sally, the jaunt was part relaxation and part anguish. All day she had been aware of a sense of approaching climax, but this evening, as sunset flamed over the pale yellow wall they were nearing, she felt differently. She would rather have been in the other car, which held five impersonal hotel residents, but even here, within a foot of Dane and inescapably a witness to Lucette's adoring glances at him, Sally knew it was good to be exploring Morocco and on the verge of discovery.

The road surface changed from the sandy gravel to huge symmetrical stones that led up to the great ornamental archway by which one entered the kasbah. Round the outside of the confining wall a few men in woollen skull-caps and dark blue djellabahs stood, presumably policing the donkey and camel traffic which meandered through the archway, laden with baskets of produce from the irrigated fields which climbed the mountainsides. In the shade of an abutment camel-drivers and labourers were huddled, counting their money and arguing, or merely chewing some never-ending sweetmeat. They watched the two big cars incuriously; no doubt the Caid had a large car of his own.

Within the walls there was a sense of peace and even beauty. The baked earth-and-stone roadway which wound round the flat-roofed houses was fringed on one side by tall hairy palms, grey-green agaves and old, rich-looking olive trees. A network of narrow cobbled lanes divided the dwellings, and along these young donkeys wandered, babies too immature for work in the fields or on the roads.

Most of the inhabitants of the kasbah wore striped robes, but here and there a very old, bearded man would be seated against the wall of his house, in flawless white. Little girls wore a long loose belted frock in almost any colour, and the boys were surprisingly Western, in shorts and striped shirts.

"They're fond of stripes, aren't they?" Sally commented. "I wish we could see more women, though; they must exist somewhere."

Pierre laughed. "They exist, certainly! The Caid has been heard to boast that the women of his kasbah are the most lovely in Morocco. There is no doubt that they wear the best materials."

"Does this place have a name?"

Pierre lifted a brow. "Did you not know we were coming to Nezam?"

Dane threw a comment and question over his shoulder. "The name wouldn't mean anything to Sally. What do you think of the place, little one?"

"It's amazing. I always thought kasbahs were primitive."

"Lots of them are, but the Caid here is an enlightened man and he has a prosperous community. The Douar of Nezam is so fertile that they're able to send large quantities of produce to Shiran and Marrakesh."

Sally repeated the name to herself. Nezam? Wasn't it the

Caid of Nezam who had a small son suffering from the after-effects of polio? Cécile Vaugard had said the man would be willing to offer a fabulous salary to anyone who could improve the child's physique even a little. Understandably, because the child was so young and the Caid did not quite trust foreign countries, he refused to send his son away for treatment. Sally found herself wondering how many people there were in wild and out-of-the-way places who went on suffering because they would not travel to find help.

Oddly, she heard herself asking, "Why isn't Mademoiselle Vaugard with us? Doesn't she care for this kind of outing?"

Lucette shot a rapier glance across the car at Sally. Dane shrugged and said, "She's been here before, and in any case she's unwilling to disappoint the customers at Le Perroquet. She promised to keep Mike company for an hour this evening."

Petulantly, Lucette put in, "Are they hatching something, those two?"

"What sort of something?" from Dane.

"I don't know. Cécile Vaugard never speaks to me, but just before we came out I saw her going from the lift to her suite. She stopped and said something about Mike knowing a lot about me. It was one of those cryptic remarks that seem point-less when you hear them and make you feel uneasy when you can't quite remember the words."

Dane laughed. "Perhaps your conscience is a little misty. Didn't wipe out your parents before you escaped from Tangier, did you?"

She tapped his hand on the wheel. "Don't be horrid. Any-way, Mike only knows my father's name in business; he's never met him."

"Mike wouldn't hurt anyone.'

"No, of course not." Lucette was comfortably willing to be convinced.

By now, they had skirted the houses and were entering the formal garden in front of the Caid's house, which was a typi-cally Moorish mansion. There were the horseshoe arches to form an arcaded terrace, mosaics halfway up the wall, and a vast carved wooden door surrounded by more highly-coloured and beautifully-patterned mosaics. The door was opened by a white-clad servant, and the whole party entered a spacious tiled reception hall whose chandelier winked in the dim light. There were mosaic-covered pillars, a fluted ceiling, a few exquisite hand-made stools covered in pale tooled leather. And in the centre of the tiled floor a star-shaped pool held goldfish; they darted among the water-vines surrounding the base of a stone flower-holder which spilled a profusion of golden trumpet-flowers. The quiet mystery and beauty of the place was enchanting.

Within a minute the Caid himself appeared, a slender figure in fine white linen which left only his brown hands and face bare. He was in his forties, a scholarly man who, during the next hour or so, asked polite questions while his servants poured mint tea and handed sweet cakes, and himself told a few anecdotes. Perhaps responsibility for the kasbah – handed down from father to son for several centuries – made him speak as if he were an old man; certainly he had acquired all the wisdom that was necessary for his task.

The correct number of glasses of tea having been consumed, Dane rose and begged the Caid to permit his guests to wash their hands. Sally and Lucette were taken in tow by a shy-looking young woman, who wore a pale pink robe and a yashmak which she dropped as soon as they had left the men. With a smile on painted pink lips and her eyes downcast, she led the way into a chamber as bare as the hall, except for a long stone wash-basin above which a couple of chromium taps supplied hot and cold water. The girl, her coffee-coloured skin showing a silvery sheen under the modern electric candelabra, stood about a yard behind them with a towel over each extended arm. Even when Sally thanked her in a polite French sentence, the Moorish girl made no reply. Possibly she knew only the Berber of the district.

Lucette went to the wide pink-tinted wall mirror and carefully made up her face. Sally finished first, and tried a little more of her French on the Moorish girl. The dark face lowered again; smilingly, the girl shook her head. And that was the only communication Sally had with the female population of Nezam.

It seemed that these parties for Europeans were conducted to a pattern. There were visits to the main souk, where everything from raw wool to finely worked metal and semi-precious stones were displayed for sale, to the little carpet workshop, to the one open-air café, which was shaded by a single palm of gigantic dimensions to the stone dyeing vats, where a late worker stirred the contents by the light of a flare, and through the gardens of the Caid's mansion. Their guide was a well-spoken young man, who was half French, half Arab, and when at last he left them in another tiled room scattered with stools and cushions, he pleasantly stated that the educational part of the evening was over. They could now enjoy themselves.

Indeed, food began to appear in immense quantities; mint tea and coffee were served from highly-ornamented silver urns, and a cabaret show, unannounced and apparently unapplauded, got under way on a small dais at one end of the room.

Rather overwhelmed by the excessive seasoning of the savouries and treacliness of the fruits and cakes, Sally drank black coffee and lay back among her cushions feeling like someone out of the Arabian Nights. Dane came and sat next to her, took her cup and placed it on a stool.

"Don't fall into a coma," he said. "I want to talk to you."

"Here?" she said blankly.

He smiled coolly. "There's a connection between the place and what I have to say. One day, before I went down to the phosphate mine, Cécile mentioned that it might do the Caid a kindness if we told him we had a physiotherapist in Shiran. He has a young son . . ."

"Yes, I know. She spoke about it to me." Sally remembered the circumstances and looked at him quickly. To Dane, apparently, it had meant little at the time. "I told Mademoiselle Vaugard that I was committed to doing my best for Mike and couldn't take on anything more."

"Did you? She didn't say." He thought it over for a

135

moment, then decided to postpone or give up conjecture. "Well, this evening I spoke for a moment about it to the Caid and he said he would like you to see the boy. He hasn't much faith in women's brains, by the way. He's had two male masseurs, who might have been quacks out to make money."

"He doesn't look the sort of man to be deceived."

"No, he doesn't." Dane added, in rather deeper tones, "The parents of an ailing child are always gullible, however educated they may be; their love makes them that way. The little boy's mother begged for a masseur, and the Caid decided it could do no harm and might do good. He told me, in confidence, that he has even called in wizards and sorcerers."

"Good lord! Do they still exist?"

"They sure do," he said laconically. "In Europe they work through television and newspapers – advertising."

"Now you're being cynical. What do the doctors say about the child?"

"The only doctor here in Nezam is a retired Moor. Everyone swears by him, and the Caid wouldn't dream of offending him by calling in a younger man, or a Frenchman. The old doctor can only be replaced after his death." An exasperated shrug. "That's how they are, and you have to accept it."

"But the Caid seems so clever and modern."

"In many ways, yes. In the things close to his heart – his women and children, and his way of living, he's still with his ancestors of two hundred years ago. I don't suppose for a moment that anything you may say will alter his ideas about the boy, but as you're here, you may as well see the youngster."

"But I'm not competent to diagnose!"

"No need for that," he said. "You've been trained to know the difference between the feel of a normal limb and an abnormal one, and I'm sure you could give a guess at what's wrong with the child."

"Is it his leg?"

"His arm, I think."

"And the legs are sound?"

"I believe so. All I really know is that the child had polio."

"Then on my own there's nothing I can do."

"You can put in a word for orthopaedic hospitals. You've had plenty of practice with Mike."

"All right." She hesitated. "Dane, it's unfair to expect me to know everything."

His look at her was cool. "Lately, I've told myself that you know so little about men and life that you ought to be well up in your profession. That's the only direction in which you seem to have used your brains."

She looked away from the unpleasant glint in his eyes.

"From the start we were wrong – you and I. You should have acted the cool and unprejudiced employer, and instead you provoked me into arguments – even about my background in England, which wasn't your business. You wanted what I could do for Mike, but you didn't take to me as a person. I can't grumble about that – you antagonized me, too. But it was wrong to allow any sort of relationship to develop. I'd have been perfectly happy just working on Mike and . . ."

"Oh, sure," he broke in roughly. "But I don't like fences between myself and those I employ, and particularly there couldn't be the barrier you wanted between me and you. You're too young and vulnerable to be allowed to go it alone in a strange country. From the very first I felt responsible for you."

"That wasn't necessary. If I hadn't been capable of looking after myself I wouldn't have come to Morocco."

"Stop it," he said softly but abruptly. "This isn't the time or the place. I'll take you to see the little boy. Give me your hand."

She did, and felt herself pulled strongly but without a jerk to her feet. The Caid, who was talking politely with a man and wife from the hotel, bowed to them ceremoniously, nodded very slightly to Dane and quietly stood back, as Dane led Sally towards him. Without a word, the man opened a door to disclose a tiled corridor strewn with hand-made rugs of distinctive design. He went ahead, opened a door into another passage which smelled of patchouli and geranium. The women's quarters, guessed Sally swiftly. But there was no sign of a woman. Even in the fair-sized room they entered there was only a man of about thirty and the child, who was small for his five years. The man rose from behind a desk, and the small boy sat up in a silk-covered bed. Either the child had not slept this evening or he had been roused some time before, so that he would be wide awake for this interview.

The Caid spoke very gently, in French. "Safia, my son, we do not come to worry you. But come from the bed and greet the guests."

The little boy with sallow skin and large dark eyes did it gracefully; slipped out on to the carpet, took a couple of paces and touched his brow and lips in welcome. Sally smiled at him, a little tremulously. He looked so small and valiant as he stood there, naked from the waist up, holding his left arm close to his body as if to support it. She knew, suddenly, that he had pain he never talked about; it was uncanny.

To the Caid, Sally said, "Is it the left shoulder, monsieur?"

He looked at her quickly, in some surprise. "Someone has told you it is the shoulder, mademoiselle?"

"No, but Mr. Ryland mentioned that the limb affected was an arm. I can see by the way he holds it that there's pain in the shoulder." She knelt in front of the child, smiled and gently pushed back a few dark hairs from his brow. In the best French she could muster she said, "You will let me touch your arm, *chéri*?"

Though it must have hurt him, he immediately turned his left shoulder towards her and dropped the arm to his side. Watching his face, Sally felt over the shoulder, saw him wince as she touched soft little lumps that shouldn't have been there. Then, turning her head so that she could not see his stoic suffering, she let her fingers probe more deeply till they felt the head of the humerus. She had forgotten the Caid and Dane.

She spoke softly, in English, with a word of French here and there. The child must have understood her tone, if not her words, for he smiled shakily, and turned so that she could feel the other shoulder. She stopped probing and held him gently, whispered that he was brave. And finally she stood up.

Dane's expression was dark and inexplicable; if anything, he looked irritated. The Caid was obviously bewildered, but his demeanour remained utterly polite.

Sally took the child's hand and led him to the bed; he climbed in and she covered him and wished him goodnight. "Sleep well," she told him. To which he nodded gravely, even though he hadn't a notion what she had said.

Sally walked out of the room, followed by the two men. The Caid's robes made a soft rustling sound as he went ahead once more and opened the doors. But he did not take them back to the reception room. Instead he opened the door of an astonishingly well-stocked library, which was certainly the brightest and gayest Sally had ever seen. There were two scarlet leather chairs, a desk and the inevitable tooled-leather stool surmounted by a gold-tasselled cushion. The Caid bade his guests take the chairs and himself sat on the stool.

"Some tea?" he asked.

"No, thank you," said Sally.

She looked at Dane and knew he would have accepted a whisky, if such a thing were available in this kasbah of non-drinkers. She didn't know why he should, but he looked fed up, so she started the conversation herself.

"Monsieur, when did your son have polio?"

It must have offended the Caid's sense of propriety that he had to talk directly to a woman, for he stared straight at the opposite wall.

"It is nearly a year ago."

"And when did the shoulder show damage?"

"About four months after. We called the doctor and he said that if the legs were not affected, the next most likely part was the shoulder."

"Was your son paralysed with polio?"

"Not after a few days. There was fever and pain all over the body, but in three weeks he was quite well again. There was then nothing . . . until many weeks later he complained of pain in the shoulder. It grew worse, and stiff. Our doctor is old, he would not touch it. Either it would clear up of itself, he said, or it was a permanent disability from the polio."

There was a silence, during which Dane shifted and made the chair creak beneath his weight. Obviously the Caïd could not bring himself to question a woman, and Dane was not in the mood just yet to help him out.

So Sally said, "I'm not competent to give an opinion, monsieur, but I think you'll find your son had polio only mildly. In paralysis, the bones go thin and brittle, but the little boy's bones are slightly larger on the left than on the right shoulder. Also, the skin in a paralysed area is bluish, but your son's skin is healthy, and on that shoulder it's the same colour as the rest of his body."

There was another silence, more tense this time. Then Dane said, with unnecessary crispness, "Go on, honey, tell us the lot. There's more on your mind, isn't there?"

The Caïd must have gained only the gist of this because it was spoken so quickly; he merely nodded. Sally felt as she had felt some time ago, when she had taken her Practical. Inwardly she trembled, but her words were clear and to the point.

"I can't tell you what's wrong with the child's shoulder, but I've felt the same condition in another child. He had a stiff and painful knee – he couldn't walk. It was discovered that the knee had been badly wrenched and never been re-set."

Dane leaned forward. "You think that may have happened to Safia's shoulder?"

She shook her head quickly. "I can't say, any more than you could. All I can say with certainty is that if he were a relative of mine I'd have him in hospital tomorrow."

Stiffly, the Caïd stood up. "You have been very good, Miss Yorke. I must thank you for the trouble you have taken."

And that was all. He took them back to the rest of the guests, Sally sat between Lucette and Pierre de Chalain and watched more acrobats, dancing girls whose chief attraction were their sequined eyelids, and a snake charmer.

She was aware of Lucette leaning towards Dane, of Dane unbending a little and laughing with her, of Pierre smothering a yawn and murmuring that it was past midnight and they had an hour and a half of driving before bed.

Then at last it was over. There were thanks on both sides, repeated again and again, the Caid bade everyone goodnight individually and took no longer over it with Sally than with anyone else. He went with them into a courtyard bathed in moonlight, where shadows were sharply etched in black and the rest was a stark unearthly white. The nine guests were ready to get into the cars.

"Most of you might like a change of driver this time," Dane suggested lazily.

"Oh, let me go with you!" begged Lucette. "I have such a ghastly feeling that I may have to leave Shiran soon, so I must make the most of it."

"With Dane?" said someone. "How outspoken can the young get!"

Dane smiled, a little tightly. "Lucette was born to flatter the male," he commented. "Pierre, you might like to take Sally in the other car and two or three of you others can come with me."

It was blatant dismissal, though none of the hotel guests was likely to realize it. Sally, feeling sick and wounded, turned straight away and got into the other car without help. She saw the silver and blue thing glide away and gather speed, smiled brightly at Pierre.

"For tonight you're my gaoler, it seems. I hope you don't mind very much."

"It is my pleasure," he said gallantly. Then he hesitated, and added very quietly, "Dane is angry about something. You are better out of his way. Mademoiselle Lucette can more easily deal with a man who is in bad humour."

Sally did not reply. She sat back as they drove away from the Caid's house, gazed without curiosity at the mysterious little lanes where donkeys still munched in the doorways and an occasional camel sat and ruminated. They passed out of the kasbah and met the loose earth of the road. The evening was over.

A couple of quiet days were a great help to Sally. She saw Mike twice each day at his house, and bathed with him in the Hotel Mirador pool each afternoon. Yes, Mike had at last consented to come again to the Mirador, though he would only bathe late in the afternoon, when the pool was almost deserted. For some reason he seemed to take a malicious pleasure in sprawling in one of the foam-rubber loungers and watching the holiday-making rich, and he always commented upon them, rather loudly. Lucette waved to them once, and he urged Sally to call her over. But Sally refused.

"While you're apart you two get along. I refuse to sit by and listen to an exchange of barbed remarks."

"But I ought to get to know the girl better before she leaves," he protested. "Perhaps I've misjudged her."

"Forget it, there's a dear. She's not very happy, you know."

Mike exaggerated his glance of surprise. "Why not? I thought she had everything – even Dane."

Sally said, rather more firmly than was necessary, "Dane's not falling for Lucette – not very far, anyway."

"A pity," he said. "I hoped he was getting it bad. Still, if she works on him for a few more days . . ." He left it at that.

Sally had never disliked a patient, but there were moments when she came near to disliking Mike. But immediately she became sorry for him, because he was torn between a desire to get whole again and a fear that the future might let him down as the past had done.

Early next morning a parcel was delivered at the hotel for Sally. It was addressed in a beautiful spidery hand, and carefully sealed. Mystified, she slit the wrapping and opened the square cardboard box. It was full of hand-made trinkets, each one swathed in a white silk square, and at the bottom of the box lay a card on which was written in French: "The Caid of Nezam instructs me to send the enclosed gift to Mademoiselle Yorke of England, and to thank her most sincerely for her kindness towards his son." There was no signature, but somehow Sally was sure that the tutor she had seen in the boy's bedroom had written the card.

She unwrapped a chased silver bracelet set with amethysts and zircons, another in the shape of a snake, with ruby eyes. There were also a signet ring, a chain necklace drooping a topaz, and several small charms made of jade and beryl. The whole must be worth quite a lot, and Sally was worried. What did one do about such a gift? It wasn't as if her advice had been welcome to the Caid; he intended to ignore it. In any case, one couldn't accept costly gifts from a stranger, whatever his position and race.

She read the card again, smiled slightly at "Mademoiselle Yorke of England." It sounded Elizabethan. Then she sobered once more, and thought about the little boy with the lumpy painful shoulder, his bravery and the pity of it all. On an impulse she gathered up the box and its contents and went along to Dane's suite. But at the door she had to collect her courage; the bright, stilted smile came to her lips and she knocked, quite firmly.

He opened the door at once, as if he had been on his way out, paused in the doorway and appraised her unsmilingly, then stepped back into the room and inclined his head to indicate that she must come in.

"Had breakfast?"

"Yes, thank you. I . . . just wondered what to do about this parcel. It's from the Caid."

She placed the box on the desk and took off the lid. The trinkets lay within, unwrapped, and Dane looked at them and picked up the amethyst and zircon bracelet.

"Pretty," he remarked briefly. Then he read the card and dropped it on top of the articles in the box. "Leave them with me, will you?"

"If you like. What will you do with them?"

"I'll thank him formally for you, and get rid of them."

"Give them away?" she said blankly.

"It's the best thing to do. The Caid doesn't realize that it isn't done for an English girl to accept this kind of thing from a stranger – but you and I understand it, don't we?"

"No, I'm afraid I don't. If I'm not returning them to the Caid for fear of offending him, the least I can do is to keep them myself, as mementoes. In fact, I'd rather like my family to see them."

"All right." He turned away. "If you'd decided what to do, why did you come to me?"

"I thought you ought to know I'd received the gift, and I wasn't sure whether it would be possible to return it. It seems I did wrong in coming here. I apologize."

But he had carelessly got between Sally and the door. "Has it occurred to you to wonder how you earned the little present?"

"I certainly didn't earn it, but he's a rich man and apparently generous. He felt he ought to pay for ignoring everything I said."

Dane shoved his hands into his pockets. "I'll tell you something. The day before yesterday, a few hours after we'd got back from the kasbah, I wrote to the Caid thanking him for his hospitality. Right at the end of the letter I invited him to come here and bring the child. That way, he could consult Dr. Demaire, and a specialist if we can get hold of one, without insulting the old doctor at Nezam. The Caid hasn't replied, even though this gift must have been brought in by messenger very early this morning."

"What do you think it means?"

"The gift? It means that the episode is more or less closed. He thanks you in the only way he knows for doing your best. In a day or two I shall receive a courteous acknowledgment of my letter, and that will be the end of it."

"The poor little scrap," she murmured. "How can a father be so blind and stubborn?"

"Stop being mawkish about someone else's child," he said curtly. "I know the way he thinks; he simply has his code and sticks to it, however foolish it may seem to us. The old doctor at Nezam has attended the Caid's family since before the Caid himself was born. To consult someone else would be dealing a death-blow to the man, and the Caid would never consent to deceive him. On the other hand, if the child were

144

threatened with death there might be some chance of moving his father . . ." He broke off, and added, in quieter tones, "Leave it to me, Sally. Keep the damned stuff if you want it, but let me handle the thanks."

"Very well," she said coolly, and took a step or two towards the door.

But it would still have been difficult to get out of the room without asking him to move or deliberately reaching across him to the handle. She curbed the quivering, and the vexation.

He took the box from her hands and placed it on the wall table near the door. Then he held her elbow and led her on to the balcony, and they looked down at a couple of early swimmers, and at the bright umbrellas above empty tables. He stood there for a moment, his expression a little jaded.

"For the first time, I'm tired of the view," he said. "Have you changed your opinion of it?"

"I don't mind it, but I wouldn't like it for ever."

"I thought not. You don't sing in the mornings any more."

She ran her finger along the stone wall. "Don't I? Perhaps I'm afraid of waking Lucette."

"Or maybe you've nothing to sing about. Yearning for Tony?"

She shrugged. "When I begin to yearn, I'll run down and see him."

"You haven't been looking too merry since he left."

"Oddly enough, I haven't been feeling it," she said. Let him make what he liked of that.

His jaw tightened slightly, his eyes looked cold as the Channel in winter. "I've had a message from Mike this morning. He says he particularly wants to give a little party at lunch-time, here at the Mirador. Know anything about it?"

"Nothing at all." She paused. "It's rather strange. Didn't he give any reason?"

He turned back to the desk and took up the sheet of note-paper. "Just a list of guests – you and me, Cécile, Lucette and himself. Says he feels like branching out, and he intends to do it in a small way to begin with. I wonder what's got into him?"

145

"Aren't you pleased that he's keen to get back into social life?"

"Of course." But the reply sounded automatic. "Why the suddenness of it, though? I've invited him here only recently, but he wouldn't come. He has something on his mind."

Sally leaned back against the door-frame of the french window and looked at him as he stood, tall and wide-shouldered, behind the desk. "I think you're right. He's going to make an announcement, and I know what it is."

"Yes?"

"Mike told me a few days ago that he was coming round to considering going to England for treatment."

"Really?" He spoke sharply and a muscle moved in his jaw. "That could be good news. Why didn't you mention it?"

"I waited till he was more certain." That wasn't the whole truth, but Sally was beginning to feel that all she had left was pride. "He made a condition. He'll go to England if I'll go too, and do my best to get a job wherever he has to have treatment."

Dane's eyes narrowed at her. For a long moment he looked dangerously male; there was even a faintly cruel twist to his lips. He asked, "What was your reaction to that?"

What had it been? Sally wasn't too sure. She moistened her lips and answered, "I don't really know. For his sake I ought to agree to it."

"And for your own?" he shot at her.

She said, low-voiced, "For my own sake I should do as Mike wants. Once he's installed somewhere and starts getting about, he'll find someone to make love to. That's what he really wants."

"Sure he does." He was about to say more, but checked himself. He flicked the letter back on to the desk, came round to face her in the opening to the balcony. "Whatever Mike has on his mind, we'll know more about it at lunch. I want you to stay away from him this morning – I'll send him a message."

"His exercises are important. I wouldn't discuss anything with him."

"You might be forced into it. I'll send him a note saying that I'll send the car for him at twelve-thirty, and that maybe he'd better rest till then."

"All right." She moved away from his nearness, felt baffled and powerless. "I'll tell Lucette about lunch, and leave you to tell Mademoiselle Vaugard. What do we do – meet down in the main lounge at a quarter to one?"

He nodded, held her glance with a controlled steadiness. His tones were hard but quiet. "Don't tell me you're not in love!"

"Very well, I won't."

"What's the agony for?" he demanded brusquely. "Having to wait two years?"

"You'd like to think that, so you may."

On a savage note, he said, "What's happened to us all? Mike's goading himself into doing something he may be sorry for, Lucette gets more excitable every day, Cécile has gone watchful and you . . . you're as brittle as Crown Derby but determined not to break."

"And you?" she queried. "Still the machine – or is it a good sign that you're getting tired of the view from the balcony?"

"Hell," he said violently, "I've had enough. If the luncheon party doesn't clear the air I'll do something about it myself. Sit down, for heaven's sake, and have some coffee!"

But Sally had stood more than enough. "I'd rather go. See you later." And she picked up the Caïd's gift and escaped before he could say another word.

In her sitting-room she drew a long breath and let out some of the tension in a sigh. She slipped the box into the cabinet and went through to the bedroom. Lucette, for once, was already up and parading in front of the mirror in her newest swimsuit – an affair in apple-green which sported a brief skirt. She pirouetted and confronted Sally.

"Like it? The skirt stays stiff in the water, but you don't swim in the suit more than necessary. It's a promenading get-up."

"Suits you. Why are you up so early?"

Lucette's lashes drooped over her dark feverish eyes. "I have to make the most of the days."

"You keep talking as if you're leaving soon, yet you won't say when."

"Because I can't, darling," said Lucette in tones of despair. "I should have left already . . . at least three days ago."

"Should you?" Sally gazed at her. "Was there a reason for it?"

Lucette nodded dismally. "A very big reason. But you know how it is for me," imploringly. "I can't bear to leave Dane."

Sally was on edge and impatient. "Then why don't you contact your parents? They can't possibly *make* you go home."

Lucette deliberately turned her back. "Unzip me, darling, and please stop reminding me that I shouldn't be here. I have to go back to utter and abysmal boredom, but I won't let it interfere with a single hour of the time that's left to me here in Shiran!"

Sally moved to her own side of the bedroom and began tidying it. After a few moments she said calmly, "We're lunching with Mike Ritchie here in the hotel today."

From the folds of an orange and white dress she was struggling into, Lucette exclaimed, "I won't meet that man! He hates me and I hate him."

"Don't be absurd. Mike wants to prove he's capable of doing the normal thing once in a while. Dane will be there."

Lucette straightened the dress over her hips. "Oh, but it's a waste, all the same. Cécile never comes down to meals and I was hoping to have Dane to myself!"

"Cécile is invited, too."

Lucette flounced towards a mirror and began to make up her face; it was painting the lily, but she managed it. With a comb in her hand she turned about.

"I've just made a decision. Cécile has to leave Shiran for Casablanca at the end of the week. I'm going to stay on over the weekend, and find out how much Dane really wants me. If he . . . proposes, I'll have all the courage in the world to face Tangier!''

Sally lifted her shoulders. It was an early hour to be tired, but she was. Tired to death of the whole tissue of duplicity and doubt.

CHAPTER NINE

THE luncheon with Mike went well. They had drinks in the lounge and talked a little, ate one of the best hot-weather meals the Mirador could produce and tasted two or three good wines with the courses. Mike had been astonishingly pleasant, Cécile had started off a little nervously but become as calm and arrogant as ever. There had been several minutes of unease about Lucette, but she stayed close to the cool, reflective Dane and his imperturbability had had its effect on her. As for Sally, she sensed the strong undercurrents of hostility, made a brave attempt to ignore them and succeeded fairly well.

They waited till the dining-room was almost empty, before getting Mike to his feet and trailing with him into a shadowed corner of the terrace for coffee. Waiters arranged a table and chairs in a semi-circle round it, and Mike was given the chair against the wall, with Sally on his right and Cécile on his left. Dane sat next to Sally and beyond him Lucette disposed herself on a lounger, to be as far as she could get from Mike.

Dane was saying, "You can rest here in the hotel, Mike, and take a bathe in the pool at your usual time or a little later." He paused, and smiled. "It's been like old times – having you here to spin a tall yarn while we eat."

Mike looked at his watch, finished the large brandy he had ordered with his coffee. "Not quite like old times. Cécile was here occasionally, but the other two maidens were busy growing out of their teens. We don't have to move yet."

"So long as you're not tired. We'll excuse the ladies, if they like."

Cécile shook her head. "Now that I am here for a meal, I will stay." She, too, consulted her watch.

Neither Sally nor Lucette made any comment at all, and Dane spoke next, about something else.

"I've been wanting to tell you some news, Mike, but I put it off till the time seemed just right. This could be it."

Mike grinned, a little tipsily. "Not going to ask me to get out of the house just yet, are you? If you're aiming to get married, I'd like a couple of weeks' notice."

"You'll get it, old chap," said Dane, with cynicism. "No, it's nothing to do with the house. When Cécile and I went to the phosphate mine, I took a few hours off and went down to the coast to see your old chief, Bruenel. I told him you were improving and he said he couldn't have heard it at a better time. The chap they took on in your place is finishing in three months, and they'd be overjoyed to get you back."

Mike's smile was unpleasant. "Really? Are you trying to stampede me into a spell in hospital?"

"No, but it's a good reason for going, isn't it? Bruenel says he'd be quite willing to carry on himself till you're ready, and he'll still go along with you for a while till you can handle things on your own again – even if it takes a year. I thought it generous of the man."

"I'm surrounded by generous men . . . and even a generous woman or two." He had looked at Cécile, not at Sally. "I'll think about it."

"Do that." Dane rubbed out his cigarette on an ashtray. "I think you, as well as the women, should rest now."

"What's the hurry?" demanded Mike pettishly. "This is the first time in a year that I've come here for lunch, and you're trying to break it up!"

"It's hot here for the girls," Dane said evenly, "and you've been drinking rather well. I'll take you through to a private lounge."

But it was Cécile who now protested. "Dane, darling, you are severe with Mike. He is happy here with us and it cannot hurt to stay a little longer. It is only three o'clock."

"I'm tired," stated Lucette firmly, without looking at anyone. "I think I'll go."

Mike wouldn't have that. He leaned over the table and stared at her long figure stretched on the lounger. "I thought you and I were friends at last," he said with smiling belligerence. "If I want you to stay, you'll stay, won't you?"

"That's enough, Mike!" Dane put in sharply. "If there's something you want to tell us, get it out, but don't pick on anyone. If you hadn't drunk more than you're used to you wouldn't be behaving like this."

Mike went bland. "What could I have to tell you? I've no secrets. Not like little Black Curls over there . . ."

Dane stood up quickly. "You're going a lot too far, Mike! We'll stop right there."

But again Cécile peeped at her watch. She looked up into Dane's face and said soothingly, "*Chéri*, this is unnecessary. Just let us sit for a minute or two in quietness. The waiters know we are here, no?"

He nodded, grimly, but did not sit down. "It's time we went our ways."

Mike sat back, blinked and said, "Cécile's right . . . just a few minutes more together and everything will . . ."

He stopped as Pierre de Chalain came along the terrace. Pierre's expression was grave and astounded. He stopped at the table, summoned a very artificial smile and spoke to Dane.

"There is a man – a stranger to Shiran – who wishes to see Mademoiselle Lucette . . ."

"Bring him here!" said Mike loudly. "Let him see all of us."

Lucette had sat up, and Sally moved swiftly, so that she could look at her. The usual high colour had gone from the creamy skin, leaving it sallow, and the black eyes stared up at Pierre in horror.

Lucette whispered, "Did the man give his name?"

Pierre nodded. "He is a Monsieur Karel Descamps, from Tangier. You will see him, mademoiselle?"

Somehow Lucette got to her feet, and Dane slipped a hand under her elbow. She turned towards him blindly, burst into tears and was held close to him for a minute. Then, with only a half-glance at those he was leaving, Dane led her shaking figure along the terrace, with Pierre at his other side. The three disappeared, and Sally became aware that her heart was thudding right through her body.

She looked at the other two, saw Mike's face, red with wine and fury, and Cécile's, faintly smiling and triumphant, and she knew that whatever had happened, they had engineered it. She wanted to get up and run away, but a frightful inertia had possession of her strength.

She said feebly, "Who is Karel Descamps – does anyone know? Is he . . . Lucette's fiancé?"

"The whole thing was spoiled," Mike said angrily. "Pierre should have brought him out here, so that we could have seen the fun. No, Sally, the man isn't Lucette's fiancé – he's her husband!"

Sally stared. "I don't believe you."

Cécile said equably, "It is true. Your vivacious young friend, who was so strictly brought up, has been married for several months to a man of forty-three. He is in business in Tangier, very rich, very sober, very proud that he has such a beautiful young wife to wear the jewels he is constantly buying for her."

"How did you find this out?"

Cécile lifted narrow, white-clad shoulders and tilted her honey-blonde head. "We made enquiries. Mike knew the name of Lucette's father, and wrote to a man in the office of the Midi Press. The reply was as you would expect to find a reply from a reporter – very concise and informative. After that, all we had to do was to send a telegram to Monsieur Descamps, asking him to catch a certain plane on a certain day if he wanted to reach his wife. He and the Millars were already frantic because Lucette was missing."

Sally managed to stand, but she was breathing as if the air in this vicinity choked her. "And you arranged this lunch, the two of you, so that Lucette could be discredited in front of Dane, and Dane made to show just how much the loss of Lucette meant to him! You wanted to sit back and enjoy the scene – only Pierre spoiled it by leaving the man in the hotel. I think you're both despicable!"

"Oh, look here," growled Mike. "There's something you haven't considered, Sally. Cécile was terribly unhappy, and when I realized that Dane was causing it because he paid so much attention to that little harpy, I felt as if I'd do anything to help . . ."

"Be quiet, Mike," Cécile exclaimed. "We do not have to explain ourselves to Miss Yorke."

He turned on her. "I wanted to tell Sally from the beginning – you know that. It was you who kept it so devilish dark!"

At that, Sally left them. She thought, 'Even thieves fall out,' and walked dazedly into the hotel lounge and through to the lift. The vestibule, as usual at that hour, was deserted, and she could hear no sound from Pierre's office. She had rung for the lift, but didn't wait for it. Taking the stairs two at a time, she arrived in the upper corridor and stood still, listening again not far from Dane's door. She thought someone was speaking in there, but could not be sure. In spite of their delicate pale blue and gold the doors were heavy and solid. Sally hesitated, and went to her own suite, let herself into the sitting-room and stood there in its emptiness, painfully aware of a thickness in her throat and a physical pain that ran down her chest towards her heart.

She clasped her elbows and walked over to the balcony and back again, saw her pink and white dress in the mirror and remembered dressing just over two hours ago, to the accompaniment of Lucette's chatter. Lucette had been happy and nervous, snatching days, even hours, of nearness to Dane, talking about it incessantly. Sally now knew why, but she couldn't think about it. She only wished she knew where Lucette was at this moment. Along the corridor with Dane and her husband? Her husband! It seemed so fantastic – Lucette married, and running away from marriage. Yet it was typically Lucette. She was a fantastic creature.

For something to do she changed into a linen skirt and white blouse, combed up her hair, hung up the things Lucette had left lying across the bed. Then it occurred to her that Lucette wouldn't want to remain at the Mirador, even if her husband were willing to do so. She would want to run away and hide from the people she had deceived.

Sally got out one of the superb blue and white suitcases, opened it on the luggage rack and began to lay in it clean undies from one of the wardrobe drawers. She had half filled the case when the outer door of the suite opened noisily and Lucette came through to the bedroom; Lucette with swollen eyelids and chastened expression, her mouth moist and trembling, her fingers twisting the grubby little strings of lace which were all that was left of an expensive handkerchief.

Sally straightened, was unable to speak first simply because she could find no words.

Lucette gulped. "All right, I know I'm bad. You don't have to tell me!" And she began flinging things into the case at a furious rate.

Sally closed the case sharply, nodded towards a chair. "Go and sit down while I pack for you. I know you feel terrible, so if you'd rather not talk about it . . ."

"But I have to talk about it! It's . . . it's an appalling thing to do – to send for Karel without my knowledge. If they'd threatened me, I'd have left Shiran and got out of their way. But they didn't say a word . . . just sent for him and arranged that we should all be together when Karel came. They told him which plane to take . . . do you know that? They even calculated how long it would take him to get from the airport to the hotel. That's the sort of people they are! And I believe you knew about it, Sally, I believe that you and Cécile and Mike . . ."

"You're worked up. You know darned well I'd never have permitted anything of this sort to happen!"

Lucette went off on another trail. "It's hurt Dane . . . hurt him so much that he could only push me into the room where Karel was waiting and leave me there. But as we walked along the terrace he did say he'd give me all the help I needed." Her voice rose, tragically. "He was as near being in love with me as he's ever been with any woman . . . and between them they ruined it – for him and for me!"

Sally's nerves were tightening again. "How could they? You're married already."

"But there might have been a chance, if I'd had time to test Dane's feelings – get him to propose."

"You mean . . . divorce?"

Lucette wiped tears from her face with a forefinger. "Divorce isn't so disgraceful when you're married to a man like Karel. He's too solemn for me, too old in his ways."

"Then why did you marry him?"

"I had to – my parents had promised him and we were almost broke. He's been good to me, but there's no excitement in being married to him, no thrills! He'd go away on business and leave me with my parents. That's what he'd done when I came here. I was bored to death at home when your letter came, and I thought I'd have a little fun and no one the wiser."

Sally began to understand. "He was in Casablanca, wasn't he? And you told your parents you were going to join him."

Lucette nodded miserably. "I'd done it once before, but it was just as dull with him as it had been at home. My mother thought it a good sign that I wanted to be with Karel for his last week or so in Casablanca, and she even helped me to pack. Sally, you don't know how glorious it was to be Lucette Millar again, and to know I could play with the men without fear. And now," her voice shook and she sobbed, "I shall never be able to do it again. They'll watch me and make me take an interest in housekeeping and acting hostess."

"That might not be a bad thing," pronounced Sally. "I've never heard of anything so irresponsible in my life. It's certainly time you grew up and learned to do your bit."

Lucette's eyes, brilliant with the tears she had shed, hardened resentfully. "You were jealous of me. You hated the way Dane laughed and talked with me, hated the fact that I was a guest in the hotel while you were only one of his employees. That was why you conspired with Mike and Cécile . . ."

"I did no such thing!"

"I believe you did."

"Because you want to believe it. In your heart you know that I'm no different from when we used to go to school together. But you're different, Lucette. The muddles you got into then were mild and harmless, and you were always sweetly and abjectly sorry if you hurt anyone. You were loyal . . ."

"If you'd kicked around the Continental for several years, trying to look good on practically no pocket money, you might have changed too!"

"But you have a rich husband now. You can't blame lack of money for the way you've behaved. I daresay you have a lovely house and garden, good friends if you'd care to cultivate them. You must have been a little fond of your husband to have married him."

Lucette said hopelessly, "I'm fond of Karel, but being fond isn't the same as being passionately in love. I've been in love a dozen times, so I know what I'm talking about!"

"Well, you got over it a dozen times, and you will again. But the man you married has the real right to your love – no one else. When you wrote to me in England about him, you called him old and horrid, but when I questioned you here, you said he wasn't so old, so your ideas must have changed. I think you need a man of his age and type; he stands a better chance than a young man would of keeping you where you belong."

"But if I could marry Dane. I'd . . ."

Sally thrust the filled suitcase on to the floor with a bang. "Put your shoes together in pairs, and we'll pack them next. And you might open the largest case close to the wardrobe, so that we can hang the dresses straight into it."

Lucette dragged herself across the room and did as Sally asked. Neither of them spoke. Lucette sniffed often and let out despairing breaths, but she did try to help with the filling of the half-dozen suitcases. Someone knocked at the outer door, and Sally opened it, to find a reception clerk there with a large envelope that bulged with Lucette's jewellery. Legacy from a grandmother, indeed!

Lucette washed her face, made up liberally and began to resemble an enamelled version of her vivacious self. But she was not herself with Sally. She ignored her. In her most bored tones she spoke through the telephone to the desk, and asked that someone be sent up for her luggage and that Monsieur

Descamps be told she was ready. She replaced the telephone, took one last look at the crumpled bedspread and the scraps of tissue paper all over the floor, picked up the large handbag and dropped the jewels into it, threw her coat over her arm and walked out of the suite.

Sally hesitated, and then followed her. Together they went down in the lift, and in the foyer Lucette paused while her cases were loaded. Her husband, a thickset man of average height and grave good looks, put her into the back of the blue and silver car. Dane appeared from somewhere, saw the unwelcome husband into the car beside her, and himself got behind the wheel. Sally's last glimpse of Lucette showed a poised young woman who looked older but slightly forlorn. In the very last moment Lucette looked her way, without hate and without affection. Dane didn't turn his head at all. He took the car at speed on to the esplanade and towards the airport.

Pierre, at Sally's side, said perplexedly, "It was quick, that. They will actually catch the plane on which Monsieur Descamps arrived this afternoon, and go back to Tangier. I have never known anything so strange!"

Pierre was too good and simple to wish for gossip on the matter. He patted Sally's arm, and moved away. Sally went along the terrace and sat down, ordered some tea. Mike had gone, of course, and Cécile was probably resting after her victory. Sally leaned back, exhausted. She felt as if she were disintegrating.

The rest of the day was ominously quiet. Sally did not go up to Mike's villa, nor did she bathe alone or eat in the dining-room. She walked some of the streets of Shiran, bought a couple of books at the hotel store – and insisted on paying cash for them – and spent the hours in her suite. She went to bed early, and was tired enough to sleep almost at once. But in the early hours she awoke, sweating and quivering, and thought about the one thing she had strictly excluded from her mind since Lucette had left.

How was Dane feeling now? Did he dislike Lucette for her

deception, or was he the more deeply hurt, because he had been in love with her? With Dane, it was difficult to judge. Falling in love happens quickly – Sally knew that, to her cost. It might have happened as precipitately to Dane, but he, of course, would have masked the emotion with mockery and banter till he was quite sure of himself, and of Lucette. Perhaps he had fallen, but despised himself a little for loving someone so volatile and undependable. Perhaps . . .

Sally turned her pillow and dug her face into its coolness. Some time she would have to talk to Dane, but she knew now, in the throbbing darkness of a Moroccan night that had lost its magic, that there would be only one talk between them, the final one. The thought of it was like dying a little.

Next morning she had to make a decision – whether to carry on with Mike as if all were forgotten or to be candid with him and tell him she would be leaving in a day or two. She breakfasted in the dining-room for a change from being alone, saw Dane as she came back through the vestibule and returned his distant greeting. She hadn't looked above the opening of his white shirt, but she was as aware of his expression as if she had stared straight into his eyes. He was cold and full of a distaste that might linger even after Sally Yorke and Lucette were unremembered in Shiran. She lowered her head and went up the staircase.

At a quarter to ten the car slipped round the drive of the villa and halted at its porch. Sally got out and entered the house, stood still in the small hall for a moment before walking slowly into the lounge. Mike was there, ostensibly absorbed in another chess problem. He looked up casually but with a furtive question in his eyes.

"Oh, hallo," he said. "I hoped you'd come. What about helping me with the problem?"

"Chess?" Sally sat down into the chair he indicated, but took no interest in the board. "Sorry, I'm not in the mood."

"I'm not, either, but I had to get interested in something, or go berserk. I was afraid you wouldn't turn up."

"I had to come at least once more."

Mike sat back and gestured. "Don't talk like that. I disgusted you yesterday, and I'm sorry. The little tramp asked for it, but I should have held off, if only because she was your friend. I did it for Cécile – I swear it."

"Partly for Cécile, but a whole lot because Lucette was the kind of girl you'd have had an affair with in the old days, and she showed her aversion to your lameness too plainly. She reminded you of the girl who let you down, and it stung."

"Yes, it did." Mike moistened his lips. "You've been thinking about it too much. What are you going to do?"

"When I arrived here this morning I wasn't sure whether to ignore the subject and give you exercises, or talk it out. But since you've waded right in, I think it's best to tell you now that I'm through with this job."

Mike didn't protest and exclaim as she had thought he might. He went gloomy and silent, and a few of the lines she had almost eradicated seemed to deepen about his eyes and mouth. He pushed a pawn across the board and a bishop after it, then rasped his bony chin with his fingers. The lock of hair fell forward and made him look rakish and unhappy.

"So I shan't be coming here any more," she said in final tones.

He nodded. "I see. It's my own fault, of course, but I wish you really understood everything. I'll admit that when I first saw Lucette I hated her brilliance and vivacity and the cowardice that wouldn't let her look at my leg. I suppose I went on hating it, but I didn't think about it much till Cécile came and told me that Dane was interested in the girl and it was making her feel wretched."

"I know it all, Mike. There's no need to go over it again."

"But I liked Cécile. Before you came, she was the only woman I spoke to. In a way, I suppose, I was grateful for her naturalness with me, and possibly even a little flattered. And then she also assured me that after she and Dane were married I could go on living in this house. She and Dane would share a suite at the Hotel Mirador. It meant quite a bit to me."

"Yes, it must have." Sally sighed. "It's odd how foolish even a woman of Cécile's experience can be. Making a public booby of the girl he . . . was attracted to wasn't the way to get Dane. Cécile need only have waited till Lucette had left Shiran."

"She couldn't afford to do that – she herself has to leave in a few days."

"But it was so ridiculous. What's love worth, if it depends on such things? If Dane realizes that Cécile was deeply involved in humiliating Lucette, he must loathe her now."

"He doesn't know, and you won't tell him, will you? Let *someone* get something out of it."

"I thought you quarrelled with her yesterday."

"I was a bit tight, and Cécile sat there smiling, though everyone else felt like hell. It got me at the time, but after I'd sobered up I decided she'd been the one who'd played it straight and I was the one who'd dithered. If anyone deserves Dane, she does."

Very coolly, Sally asked, "But does Dane deserve Cécile? I'd say he deserves someone a trifle more honest and loving."

"You might be right," he said helplessly. "It's a pity Lucette Millar . . . Descamps, or whatever her name is, ever came to Shiran."

"It was through me. I haven't done much good here, have I?"

Mike met her glance squarely, for the first time. "You've done me good – plenty of it. You made me realize that all girls aren't alike, that there are a few sweet, dedicated ones, who'll see a thing through, even if it's not too pleasant."

"You've been pleasant enough," she said, "but I didn't come here with the object of curing you. Dane told me to work on you both ways, but he stressed that the most important thing was to persuade you to go to England for treatment. I agreed with him." She paused. "You've recovered from that girl who couldn't bear to stay with you after your accident, haven't you?"

"Yes, I've recovered."

"It wouldn't worry you a great deal if you meet her again?"

"The way I feel now," he said bitterly, "I'd laugh in her face."

"Then you're ready to go to England?"

Again Mike's tongue stole along his lips. "I'd have gone to England with you at any time during the last couple of weeks."

"And now you're willing to go without me?"

"You've been talking to Dane!"

"No, we haven't spoken together since yesterday at lunch."

Mike looked his disbelief, said sourly, "He came here yesterday evening and said he'd arranged for Dr. Demaire's young assistant to escort me to England. I apologized for what had happened, but he said it wasn't enough; I had to show my regret in a tangible way – put myself in the hands of an orthopaedic man in Britain. He wasn't nasty – just icy cold and implacable. I didn't answer and he walked out."

"But you'll go?"

"How can I hold out . . . now?" His hand clenched on the squared table. "I've never told you this, but you may have guessed it. I was a spender – got my money easily doing what seemed like child's play, and spent it the same way. After the accident I hadn't a sou. I told you I'd take you on if Dane let you go, but the truth is I'd have had to pay your salary with money that Dane had paid into my account. For nearly a year now I've been living on him. He paid the hospital expenses, let me live here, got everything for me I could possibly need." He hesitated. "Knowing that, perhaps you can understand why I resented him. It's a strange truth that you dislike those who are most lavish with assistance. Yet what I'd have done without Dane to back me up and bark at me, I don't know."

"So you're realizing that he merits a little gratitude?"

"Yes, but not for the money it's cost him – but because he brought you here. You got me on my feet, Sally. You made me swim and laugh and make it up with Tony." His voice went thin. "I wish I'd been more . . . considerate."

She gave him a pale smile. "That's all right, Mike. I've done what I was engaged to do, and you can go on exercising on your own, till you get into competent hands in England. I hope you'll let me know how you get on. You can write to the farm; I'll be somewhere near."

"Won't you come here and see me again?"

"Better not." She got up from the chess table. "Can I get you anything?"

"No, thanks."

"You won't be difficult with Dane?"

"Probably," with the ghost of a grin, "but I'll do what he wants, just the same." He touched his neck. "I'm fed up to here with fighting the man. Reluctantly, I give in."

"Good." She went slowly towards the door. "This time next year you'll be a journalist again and choosing a new car. Make it a sedate one this time; they get you there just the same. Goodbye, Mike."

"So long, Sally," he said, rather sadly. "And good luck."

She came out into sunshine that stung her eyes, blinked rapidly for a few seconds and went down to the car.

It is an incontestable fact that when difficulties and problems begin at last to resolve themselves they often do so with bewildering speed. On her way back to the Mirador that morning Sally felt as if a small weight had been lifted from the load she bore. Lucette was gone, the task of persuading Mike was complete, and she was free to consider the next step. She went up the wide marble steps into the hotel, glanced incuriously into the lounge and saw Dr. Demaire seated in a deep armchair and in close converse with . . . the Caid. Involuntarily she hesitated, and in that moment the Caid raised his head and saw her. Swiftly, he stood up and bowed, came to meet her with Dr. Demaire just behind him.

"I have been hoping to see you, mademoiselle, in order to thank you in a proper manner for your little examination of my son."

"You've thanked me already, monsieur. Your gifts left me breathless!"

He smiled, showing strong, yellowish teeth. "So I have heard, from Mr. Ryland. He came out to Nezam very late last night, and we motored back together arriving here at dawn with my son."

Sally shelved her troubles, and smiled delightedly. "So that Dr. Demaire could see him? I'm so glad!"

"I, too, mademoiselle. It seems it will be necessary for my son to enter the clinic here, but there is no doubt that it was an undetected injury and not the polio which caused the bad shoulder."

"That's wonderful news."

Sally did not ask about the old doctor of Nezam, or what inducements Dane had used to get the Caid to bring his son to Shiran. She smiled again, murmured more conventional words of delight and allowed herself to be bowed into the lift.

That afternoon she packed most of her clothes. Two things were still on her mind, the most painful of them the unavoidable interview with Dane. She would have liked to get it over, yet shrank from the inevitable strain of the hours which would follow, while she waited for a seat on the plane. For a phone call had elicited the fact that she could only be sure of leaving in two days' time; there might, though, be a cancellation which would enable her to leave tomorrow. Sally thought about it, and then rang the agent to confirm that she would definitely be leaving on the plane for which she had made a provisional booking. She had two days in which to settle her disordered mind, live through a short interview with Dane and say her few goodbyes.

That evening the guests of the Hotel Mirador were given a surprise. A small concert was held in one of the lounges after dinner, and the main artiste was the celebrated French mezzo-soprano, Cécile Vaugard. Sally slipped into an armchair just as the lights dimmed, and she listened to Cécile with an odd sort of detachment. A good voice, she conceded, one that fell only a little short of the highest operatic standards; Cécile was best in the ballads, because they demanded a stereotyped brand of emotion, but the audience gave loudest applause to the popular love songs about Paris, with which the recital finished.

The lights went up, Sally sat on for half an hour and then went up to bed. But as she left the lift in the upper corridor, Dane came from his suite. For a second she thought he wouldn't do more than incline his head; but he stopped.

"You've heard about the Caid's son?" he asked abruptly.

"Yes, it's marvellous news."

"The child is already in the clinic." A pause. "Not curious as to how I got them here?"

"Yes, of course."

"I used a bit of friendly licence," he said. "Told the Caid that I'd discovered it was possible the boy's shoulder might be infected, that it might gradually kill him. After that he didn't need much persuasion."

"You thought it up that day when you discussed it with me?"

He nodded. "It occurred to me . . . but other things happened, and I didn't come round to acting on it till late last night. I might have left it till this morning, but I thought the whole thing might seem more urgent if I tackled the Caid fresh from his bed, in the small hours."

"Good psychology," she commented. "The shoulder isn't infected, of course. Infection doesn't remain static for months at a time, and you know it."

"Maybe the Caid didn't know it – or he allowed himself to forget it, because it created a loophole in his rigid code. After a great deal of thought he's decided to give his own old doctor a trip to Mecca."

She made a slight movement towards her door. "It seems all set to end well, anyway," she said.

He glanced at her keenly. "If it hadn't, the child would have stayed on your mind, wouldn't he?"

"Yes. Yes, he would."

"Then you might as well thank me. I did it as much for you as for the boy."

"For me?"

Cynicism entered his tones. "I was there when you saw the child – remember? I can't stand women who cry, but that night I discovered that even less can I stand women who want to cry and won't. Funny, isn't it?"

Through dry lips she said, "Well . . . thank you."

"Nothing more to say?"

"About the boy?"

"About anything."

She lifted her shoulders. "Not much, just now. I enjoyed Mademoiselle Vaugard's concert."

"As much as you enjoyed Lucette's mortification yesterday?"

She winced, as if from a physical blow, and suddenly her young face was lean and shadowed. The news of Lucette's marriage must have wounded him deeply, for him to speak like that. She turned away and left him, went into the suite and locked the door behind her. All that now remained to be said to Dane could be put into a brief note. It had been as simple as that.

When she awoke next morning the day stretched in front of her, empty and melancholy. And almost at once she decided what to do with it. She had coffee and a roll in her room, put on one of her prettier dresses – white and turquoise with a flyaway collar – and went downstairs to seek out Monsieur de Chalain. He was in his office, reading the local newspaper, but as usual he jumped to his feet and beamed upon her, offered her a chair and wanted to know if she would like mint tea or something cold.

"Nothing as early as this, thank you, monsieur," said Sally, as she sat down. "You're very peaceful in here."

"The sound-proofing. Dane insisted on it, for my nerves, and I have been grateful many times." He twinkled. "One can enjoy the newspaper or one's favourite gramophone record without risk."

It was easy to talk to Pierre. Sally found herself saying at once, "I haven't told anyone yet, but I'm leaving Shiran the day after tomorrow."

"But that is calamitous!" He looked as though he meant it, too. "You seem to have been with us such a short time, mademoiselle, yet you have meant a great deal to several of us. You know," wryly humorous, "I wanted you for a daughter-in-law from the moment we met. It was not to be, but I would still have liked to keep you here, perhaps having some good times with the guests and . . . I admit it . . . with Tony and myself. You are happy to be leaving us?"

She shook her head but contrived a smile. "I can't say that, but I'll do my best to settle down again at the Beckmoor."

"To be young is to be resilient," he said. "I envy you. And now I must get Tony here to say goodbye to you. Dane has forbidden him to come to Shiran before the month is up, but he would not mind his coming for that, I think."

"Well," she said uncertainly, "I thought I might go out to the plantation and see him today. I know it's considered un-conventional for a girl to do such things in this country . . ."

"But you are English, and so to some degree is Tony!" Pierre exclaimed. "Go to the plantation by all means. He will give you lunch and you can speak together about this im-portant matter of the kitchen, no?"

She nodded. "But there's the question of transport. I don't want to ask for the hotel car – I might keep it too long, anyway. Would you trust me with your own car, monsieur?"

He said whimsically, "I have already said I would trust you with my son, mademoiselle. You shall certainly have the car. But are you sure you know the way to the plantation?"

"I've been there only once, but you can tell me again. I'm very grateful, monsieur."

It was ten-thirty when Sally eventually left the Hotel Mirador in the ponderous vehicle which, in spite of Moroccan dust, Monsieur de Chalain kept black and gleaming. For several miles she had no need to consult his directions, and after she was accustomed to the heavy gears she drove without strain.

It was about fifteen minutes past twelve when she turned

down the lane which was signposted in new black letters on a white ground: "L'Espérance. Antoine de Chalain."

L'Espérance! Hope . . . the most precious coin in the world. And there was Tony coming from the house, shading his eyes and staring into the familiar car, expecting to see his father. But within a second or so he recognized her, and gave a whoop of joy which she heard as she switched off the engine.

How good to be away from the Mirador and with Tony, who knew nothing whatever of the turmoil and distress of the past days. Sally smiled at him and gave him her hand.

CHAPTER TEN

For an hour Sally walked among the date palms, watched lithe, dark-skinned workers climb the trunks and snip the great golden bunches of dates, and listened to technical problems which left her no wiser about date cultivation than she had been before.

"The yield is poor," Tony said earnestly. "Good dates, but not nearly enough of them. We have to nurse the trees along for a while and plant new stuff where the dead palms have been cut out. Devil of a job to root out a palm, you know. The first one took us a whole day, but after that I had to plan a routine. We're getting along much quicker now."

"Is it going to be a success, Tony?"

"Sure is. In a year or two I'll be able to buy the old man a new car."

She smiled. "He's so pleased for you. I do like your father, Tony."

"Hey, now!" But his grin was happy. "I like him, too. Can you stay to lunch?"

"That was the idea. A sandwich will be enough."

"We can do better than that. My right-hand man is a peasant type who grows vegetables. The servant always cooks too much for me, and in any case, you're welcome to my share if you can manage it. Believe it or not, apart from my father you're my first visitor."

"Hasn't Dane been over?"

"No, he's coming just before the first month is up, to see how things are going. That's soon enough for me! Like a wash?"

"Yes, please."

He took her into a bare kitchen, where a youth dressed in white shorts, a turban and nothing else was stirring a pot over an old wood stove. Tony gave her some soap and a towel, nodded towards the sink.

"The bathroom isn't quite ready yet, but it's coming along. I take my nightly tub in here or out on the veranda. It's all very makeshift, but I don't mind it."

She soaped her hands and rinsed them. "Everyone thought you'd find it hard to live in these conditions. I'm glad you don't."

"Nothing hard in watching a daily improvement in the house. I wouldn't mind seeing some life in the evenings, but I'll stick it out. Finished? Then come into my living-room. I sleep there, too, but we keep it tidy."

The room was large and rather crowded with odd pieces of furniture which must have been spared from the hotel; they included a single bed and a wardrobe, as well as normal lounge furniture. The table had been arranged near the low window, and already the servant was setting another place and pulling up a chair. A few minutes later he brought in large fried chops which Sally suspected were goat's meat, a mound of onions surrounded by mashed potatoes, and another dish of mixed vegetables which consisted of a base of lima beans, a layer of diced carrot and a topknot of minced cabbage.

"He does you well," Sally commented, after the servant had left them. "The meal looks most appetizing."

"He was trained at the Mirador," replied Tony complacently. "Kitchen-boy, who was very observant. Help yourself."

They had left the table and were drinking coffee in the armchairs, when Sally decided it was time she gave Tony the various pieces of news. She began with Lucette, but omitted mention of Mike and Cécile. Tony's mouth fell wide as he listened, but he was silent till she had ended with, "So Lucette went back to Tangier with her husband. I hope she'll forget it all and be happy."

"But what a fool she was," he exclaimed. "She couldn't have been so sophisticated, after all. How did her husband know where to find her?"

Sally sipped her coffee. "Someone informed him – apparently a tip from Shiran."

"It must have been a bit of a knock for Dane."

"Yes, I think it was," she said quietly, "but he'll get over it. He may even marry Cécile."

Tony said sympathetically, "It hurt you a little, didn't it? You're not looking so merry as you used to. Are you still working hard on Mike?"

"That's another thing I have to tell you. Mike's consented to have treatment in England."

"The deuce he has! You *are* a fast worker. When is he going?"

"Fairly soon – and I'm leaving Morocco myself in a couple of days."

Tony lost his smile. "Darn it, I wish you wouldn't go yet. Just knowing you're not far away in Shiran gives me a boost; I'm still a bit weak on self-assurance. Will you come back some time?"

"I doubt it. Don't let's talk about it." She put down her cup. "I brought some magazines with illustrations of kitchens in them. They're in the car."

"I'll get them. We've a very good carpenter on the job – he's working on the back windows at this moment – and there's plenty of wood, so you can choose any design you like. I want a really good kitchen, because I may hitch up one day – you never know."

"Of course you will."

But left alone for a few minutes, Sally became aware that her heart was heavy and slack. She could imagine a woman in this place, teaching the servant new dishes, arranging and re-arranging the furniture throughout the house till she was quite satisfied, making a flower-box for the veranda, singing to herself while she sewed, and laughing at life with Tony. He wasn't a dream-man by any means, but a girl who loved him could be gaily happy with Tony de Chalain.

Sally wondered about the balcony upstairs, thought it must have been repaired, or she would have noticed it as she arrived. Tony would have been surprised to learn that, in the days to come, the balcony of his house would provide one of her most vivid memories of Morocco. Even at that moment, when his returning footsteps sounded on the tiles in the hall, Sally could feel herself back up there, sprawled over the floor with Dane's arm like a vice about her ribs, while his other hand bled thickly from the graze. She could see the fury in the sea-green eyes, hear the rasp of his breath as he let her go.

She got up quickly and went to meet Tony. "Let's go into the kitchen and plan it," she begged.

Tony looked at her curiously. "I'll get some sketching paper and we'll do it properly."

In the kitchen they talked, sketched and made decisions for nearly two hours. Then Sally thought she must leave; as she was driving the car, she wanted to get back to Shiran before dark. Tony shoved a kettle on the stove, found some rubbery biscuits and fresh sweet cakes concocted by his gem of a cook. Sally made tea, English fashion, and it was just after four-thirty when they both came out to the car.

Tony patted the bonnet. "She irritates me, but bless her for bringing you. Eats up the petrol, though, doesn't she?"

"I don't know – I didn't look."

Tony peered in at the dashboard, switched on the ignition and peered again. "The tank is less than a quarter full. That won't get you home."

"Won't it? What shall I do?"

"Did you fill up before you came?"

"Your father told someone to fill the tank, but I didn't see it done, and I'm afraid I didn't check the indicator, either. Don't you have any petrol here?"

"I've a little in a can. I use a spot to start up the tractor, but after that it runs on paraffin." He paused and meditated. "With what you have left and my gallon you can do about forty miles. It's seventy-eight to Shiran."

"And not a petrol pump on the way!"

"There's one due west of here – about thirty miles away. I could take you there and fill right up, but you'd have to drop me back here and travel on in the dark. Somehow I think it would be better for you to go straight towards Shiran."

"What about the other plantations? Doesn't anyone run a car?"

"The roads are not tempting. In this district they use horses." He nodded suddenly. "I've just thought of something. You remember the olive orchards about halfway here? A Frenchman owns them and I know he has a lorry. I'll go with you that far and see him for you, then send you on your way tanked up. I can get back here under my own steam."

"Thank heaven you thought of that. Sorry, Tony."

"That's all right. It means I don't have to say goodbye to you yet!"

The sun was already well down when they left the plantation. Gold dust lay over the miles of arching green branches and the distant mountains were a blur of purple and yellow outlined in flame. Plantation workers straggled to their grubby stone dwellings, a desert coolness came on the breeze and plumes of smoke began to rise into the sunset. Sally, sitting beside Tony, knew a wrenching sadness, a desperate premonition of loneliness. A few weeks ago she would have said it was impossible to feel part of this country and the people she had known a comparatively short time, but now she had to admit a need to belong here that was frightening in its violence. It was unbearable.

At about this time, in Shiran, Pierre de Chalain was looking at his watch, and wondering. Ten-thirty in the morning till six at night covered rather more hours than were appropriate for a young woman to be alone at the house of a young man. Of course, these English were extraordinary; indeed, it was known that a couple could be friendly for weeks without even attempting the most casual embrace. But Tony wasn't all English, and that made this particular couple slightly different. He would be glad when Miss Yorke returned.

From his office he spoke over the telephone to the reception desk. "The Caid has left?"

"An hour ago, monsieur."

"And Monsieur Ryland has returned from the airport?"

"He is here now."

"*Bien*. You will tell him that the samples have arrived from the mine – that they are here in my office."

Pierre rang off, clipped a cigar and poured an apéritif. He was in the act of lighting the cigar when Dane came in.

"A drink, *mon ami*?"

"Thanks. Make it whisky." Dane cast a jaded eye over the half-dozen tightly-wrapped rock samples. "I'll get someone to call for them, for analysis. Do you mind having them in here till tomorrow?"

"Not at all. Soda?"

"A splash." Dane tried the drink, put it down and shoved his hands into his pockets. He walked over to the window and looked out at an angle of dark garden. "Sometimes, Pierre, I feel as if I'll get out of this hotel, for good."

Pierre showed consternation. "But no! While you remain unmarried you are part of the Mirador." Then he smiled. "Drink up, my friend. It will help you to feel less lonely, now that Cécile has gone. The plane was late to leave, it seems."

"Engine trouble. We had to kick around for a couple of hours. It was wearing."

"Naturally. Cécile would have arrived in Casablanca as quickly by road. She has made the usual new contract with Le Perroquet?"

"No, she hasn't."

The uncompromising negative left Pierre a little dazed, but he nodded agreeably. "She could have it if she wished, I am sure. She sings like a nightingale, that one."

"That's a little trite and not exactly true, but you mean well." Dane finished his drink and turned towards the door; there, he paused and said in non-committal tones, "They told me at the desk that Miss Yorke telephoned the travel agent – twice. Know anything about it?"

"Mademoiselle said nothing to me. I know she is leaving, of course, but no details."

Dane went oddly still. "Leaving? She actually said so – to you?"

Pierre said quickly, "It was only this morning. You cannot have seen her since then."

"No, I've been out most of the day."

Dane moved suddenly towards the door, and Pierre hastened to ask, "You go up there now – to see her?"

The reply came through tight lips. "I've more right than anyone else to know what she's up to. It's bad enough being chased up by the Caid and having to spend futile hours at the airport, but I'm damned if I'll let . . ."

"Just a moment!" Pierre was anxious. "Miss Yorke is not in her room. She is out. This morning I gave her permission to use my car. She left for the date plantation to say goodbye to Tony."

Dane said something that Pierre thought it wiser to ignore, and demanded swiftly, "And she's not back? What time did she leave?"

"Mid-morning."

"Did she say when she'd return?"

"No, but it was agreed that she would stay with him for lunch. You need have no concern about the car, Dane. It may be old, but always I keep it in first-class condition. Miss Yorke is not a careless one. She would not drive too fast."

"But she's alone?"

"Yes. I must confess I feel she should have arrived here while it was still light, but you know how it is with the young. They will wait and talk and miscalculate . . ."

"You shouldn't have let her have the car! I haven't allowed her to drive in Morocco."

"But she can drive, so why not in Morocco? She asked me, because it was the only way she could see Tony."

"Damn Tony," said Dane, unforgivably, and he swung open the door and went out.

But Pierre was not affronted; he was concerned and puzzled. Always, during their association, Dane had been friendly, if sometimes abrupt. Never had he looked as he had a moment

175

ago, pale with anger . . . and something else. Assuredly, the imperturbable and masterful Dane was involved in something catastrophic. Being a Frenchman, Pierre drew but one conclusion.

Dane, meanwhile, had stalked out to the blue and silver car and got back into his seat. He seemed to have been driving and trying to hang on to his temper all day, but now he let go, started the car and swung it out on to the esplanade, accelerated up to a cool sixty, even within the city limits. And naturally, it was not long before he left Shiran behind him. There was little traffic on the road, and that little consisted chiefly of donkey carts and an occasional small military car heading for the lights of Shiran. He would know Pierre's car a mile away by its gargantuan headlights. Pierre maintained that the bigger the beams, the more likely it was that other cars would be well out of his way before he reached them. He could be right.

Dane's right foot went down hard, the car touched eighty, eighty-five. It held the road at that speed for twenty minutes and then, fortunately, the surface undulated for a stretch and he had to lose speed; otherwise he would have shot past the car on the verge without noticing that it was Pierre's. But he did notice; he braked and reversed, slipped out to examine the vehicle. The lights were off but the bonnet was still warm; on the front seat lay a white straw hat that he recognized. Dane slammed the car door, stood back and looked about him. Wild thicket and olive trees beyond; certainly no place for a girl to explore alone. She had taken the car keys with her . . . or maybe – a sweat dewed his temples – she had been stopped by someone. Not that highway violence of any kind had ever been heard of in these parts, but there always had to be a first time.

He sounded the klaxon of his own car, waited a minute and did it again. No response of any kind. But wasn't there a small light bobbing away among the trees? He made for it along a narrow, thorn-strewn footpath, came face to face with a small brown man in a soiled djellabah who carried something in each hand, as well as the torch.

Dane spoke at once in French. "Have you seen a white mademoiselle?"

The bewildered peasant stared up at the big Englishman. "Yes, monsieur. She is at the house of the olive farmer."

"Unhurt?"

"Yes, monsieur. The car had no petrol – it stopped just there on the road. Monsieur will see that I carry two cans of petrol."

Dane muttered automatic thanks, patted his shoulder and got into his own car. He drove slowly, looking for the turn, took it and saw the small farmhouse in the distance. She had walked this, he thought grimly, walked it in the darkness. But how had she known a house existed among the trees? It wasn't visible from the road.

By the time he reached the cottage the burning anger and anxiety had become transmuted into something less easily definable. He stood on the path, was on the point of taking the last pace to the door when he paused, to look into the simple room illuminated by a paraffin lamp. The swarthy little farmer was in there, nodding and waving his pipe as he talked. Sally sat in a wooden rocking chair, drinking something from a large mug, and right next to her, with his elbows on the table, lounged Tony de Chalain. Taut as steel, Dane gave one terrific thud on the door and flung it open.

For an endless moment the three inside the room stared at him as he stood there, big, lean and almost threatening, in the doorway. Then, very carefully, Sally put her cup on the table and Tony stood up.

"Hi, Dane," he said awkwardly, and with a weak attempt at flippancy. "Fancy seeing you here."

"Yes, fancy." Dane sounded as if he could hardly trust himself to say more, but he went on, "I understand you ran out of petrol."

"Yes, that's right. I was going to see Sally on her way from here and hang about till I could hitch a ride back towards the plantation."

"You needn't hang about," Dane said curtly. "Use your father's car, and come up to Shiran in it at the weekend. I'll take Sally." He turned to the olive farmer. "Very many thanks for all you have done, monsieur. I'll see that you're paid."

"But it was nothing, Monsieur Ryland. I was happy to be of assistance."

"We're very grateful."

Without another word he got Sally outside, took her arm and marched her to the car. They were on their way within a minute, Sally having uttered no word since his sudden arrival. Dane didn't look at Pierre's car as they shot past it, and Sally didn't dare to mention her hat.

At last she did say, "It wasn't anyone's fault. Monsieur de Chalain told someone to fill the tank, but they could only have put in a few gallons. If Tony hadn't looked at the indicator, I'd have been stranded on my own. When he saw how low the fuel was, he wouldn't let me go alone. We actually made for the olive farmer's place, but the petrol ran out about a mile off."

"Leave it," he said brusquely.

"You can't blame anyone."

"I'm not blaming anyone."

"Back at the cottage you looked as if you thought Tony was at fault. He wasn't."

"All right, you've put Tony in the clear. Now be quiet!"

And she was. In any case, you can't argue with a man while he's driving like a maniac. They swept down into Shiran, pulled up in the courtyard of the Hotel Mirador. Dane was opening her door before Sally had realized they had arrived, and the next moment he was propelling her through the vestibule and into the lift. Oddly, she wasn't a bit surprised to be pushed along the corridor and into his sitting-room. He was in a mood to do almost anything.

Luckily the telephone rang and gave her a minute's respite. It was Pierre, apparently; he must have seen them come in.

Dane said, "Yes, it's all right – tell you about it later. Tony has your car till the weekend, by the way. No, nothing's wrong with it. Right." He rang off, picked up the phone again and ordered drinks.

Then he took off his jacket and tossed it on to a chair, turned about and stared at Sally. She withstood the scrutiny for what seemed a long time, then looked away.

"Do you mind if I go now?" she asked politely.

"I've a few things to say to you. Take a seat."

Sally remained standing. "I suppose Monsieur de Chalain told you I'm leaving the day after tomorrow. I was going to let you know myself this evening."

"That would have been nice – to have you actually coming along to give me the news. Or were you going to write me a little note?"

Sally didn't answer that; the sarcastic remark was too perceptive. "My work here is finished. It was obvious I'd be leaving soon."

"But I brought you here, and it was up to me to book your passage home. You were due to remain here at least until Mike goes."

"There was no reason for it, and I didn't want to."

"Not even to be near Tony for a bit longer? I seem to recall that when I asked you if you were yearning for him you said that when you began to yearn you'd go down and see him."

"Oh, stop it, Dane." For the first time her voice shook. "I went to the plantation to say goodbye."

"It took you a long time."

"I stayed because I liked it there! Tony was restful, which is more than you can say about anyone here. Even Pierre is often infected with the Hotel Mirador unrest."

"And you can't wait to leave Morocco!"

Sally lifted a hand. "I don't belong here, as you seem to. I . . . I know you're feeling pretty terrible, and I also know that I'm half responsible for it . . ."

"Half!" he ejaculated unpleasantly. "You're the whole works, honey."

"That's not fair. It was through me that Lucette came here, but the rest was up to you. If anyone had suggested that you'd fall in love with her and get hurt I'd have thought it the joke of the year, but..."

"And it would have been. Lucette is a charming idiot and as unstable as they come. To me, until that last day, she was just that – an attractive little joke."

"I don't believe it," Sally said flatly. "You've behaved like a humourless bear since she left."

"I've felt far worse than that," he returned forcibly. "How could you lend yourself to that plan of Mike's? I know you did nothing to further it – you're not capable of that – but you knew what was going to happen to Lucette, your own friend! You let her lounge there on the terrace waiting for a disaster of which she had no inkling. Even if you knew only a little, you should have warned her."

"But I knew nothing!" Sally retorted. "I was as much taken by surprise as she was. I didn't speak because I was afraid of worsening matters. How dare you think I'd harm Lucette! You... you..."

"Hold on!"

She turned furiously away as the steward brought the tray of drinks into the room. Dane waved him away and began pouring, but the moment the door had closed he set down the bottle and turned to her.

"Lucette had a word with me while her husband was attending to the luggage at the airport. She said you practically admitted knowing what Mike and Cécile were up to."

"I knew nothing whatever. Why should she say that?"

"God knows," he said savagely, and took a turn about the room. "Unless... well, unless she was afraid I had too good an opinion of you."

Sally's mouth was dry. "Lucette doesn't think of me like that."

Dane's manner had changed a little. "You really hadn't any notion at all of what Mike was planning?"

"None."

"Well," with an angry sigh, "that's a relief, anyway. It was a comparatively small thing, but it was there, a little wound that kept getting rubbed. I didn't want to believe it, but I didn't see that Lucette had anything to gain by lying."

"She was hurt and humiliated – and I wasn't as sympathetic as I should have been. I suppose I was too shocked at the way she had treated the man she married." She paused, bit at the inside of her lip. "Then you didn't . . . really care for Lucette?"

"Heavens, no," he said impatiently. "She was gay, and at the end I must admit I felt sorry for her. Her husband seems a good chap, but he'll be stern with her from now on. She needs it."

By now, Sally was a little dazed and worn. "Do you think we might have that drink?"

He gave her a glass containing a spot of gin, topped it with orange and ice and then poured whisky for himself. He lifted his glass and said, "To honesty. I can use some from you right now." And he tossed off half the drink.

She sipped gratefully, and knew that the tiny proportion of gin could not possibly be responsible for the cautious little glow within. She had been wrong about his feeling for Lucette. Was it possible . . . ?

He asked bluntly, his eyes watchful, "Had you said goodbye to Tony before I arrived?"

"No. No, I hadn't."

"No kisses at the plantation?"

"Not one. Tony and I aren't that way about each other. I wish there were some way of convincing you."

"There is," he said tersely.

"Is there?"

"You could tell me there was someone else."

A silence throbbed between them. Sally's glass was taken from her fingers and she looked up quickly into the lean clever face gone dark with some emotion, into eyes in which the banked-down fires had suddenly flamed. She felt the flexible strength of his fingers upon her upper arms. The dark cloud of torment in her own eyes cleared magically and her breath caught in her throat.

"For Pete's sake," he said thickly. "Don't look at me so

meltingly unless you mean it. I've stood enough agony from you, young Sally."

She whispered, "What did you mean – someone else?"

"Do I have to translate it into words of one syllable? Can't you . . . feel it?"

She did, then. Felt it tingling through his fingertips, surging up from her own heart. Trembling, she pressed her face against him and clung, and for a long time there were just his hands, moving and gripping over her back, and the leaping responses of her own nerves. Then he lifted her chin and looked into her eyes, and she was filled with a painful rapture as his mouth came down to meet hers.

Some time later Dane said, "You earned that bonus, little one. We'll make it a trousseau after all – let ourselves go in Paris."

"Paris!"

"On the way to England. I suppose you'll insist on getting married in Cumbria?"

"Oh dear," she said, going scarlet. "Do we have to think about marriage? It's a bit soon, when we've only just kissed for the first time."

"But *how* we kissed!" He laughed at her expression. "Haven't been in the habit of doing that kind of thing with other chaps, have you?"

"No, but . . ."

"Like to know that we'll kiss like that every day for the rest of our lives, wouldn't you?"

"Yes, but . . ."

"There's only one way to make sure of it. Hook the guy." He rubbed his cheek against her hair. "I love you, Sally. I was never more certain of anything in my life. That day you nearly crashed down from Tony's balcony I knew I had to marry you – look after you for ever. That's why I was so furious with you. In a matter of seconds I knew I loved you and nearly lost you. God, it was appalling."

"But it was after that that you kissed Lucette!"

"She kissed me," he reminded her, "but I didn't object, as

you were watching. We'd just had a row on the terrace, if you remember."

"I remember everything."

"Good. Perhaps you now realize why I was so keen to get Mike on the go in England. He's all right, but I wanted him out of our way."

"Tony, too?"

"Tony most of all," he said, sounding grim. "I knew what you felt for Mike was professional compassion, but Tony's pleasant and quite a good-looker, and he does mean to succeed with the plantation. He's wasted a lot of time, but he was steadying up a little before you came, and I was horribly afraid his situation would appeal to that touchingly soft heart of yours. Why was it never soft for me?"

"I had to protect myself."

"Against what?"

"The machine," she said tremulously. "It's only very recently that I've believed you could love anyone, and then I was so afraid it was Lucette. I didn't want to fall in love with you."

He laughed, exasperatedly. "I knew that the moment we met. You were a young woman out of England for the first time, yet you refused to be impressed by Morocco or anything else. You took one long blue-eyed stare at me and decided that Morocco had nothing on Cumbria and that you would do your job and get out, quick! Like it or not, my darling, you fell the whole way that first day, just as I did – I haven't felt right since. But you were a sight more stubborn about acknowledging it."

"Not to myself," she said softly.

"That's something." He hardened and let her go. "It'll take me ages to recover from the shock of knowing you were arranging to leave. How did you expect me to react to that?"

She looked up at him, beseechingly. "Dane, I didn't know how you felt, but now that I do know . . . I'd never do anything to hurt you; I'd hurt myself so much more. You're such a strange man . . ."

"Don't say that!"

"Nice strange," she qualified. "You do such a lot for everybody in such an odd and cold way. I'm sure there's no other man in the world who'd have gone off to the kasbah at Nezam in the middle of the night to scare the Caid into bringing his son to Shiran! And do you know what I believe? You first took over the Mirador because you liked Pierre . . . and you backed the date plantation for the same reason."

"I did that for you. It was the first piece of Morocco that you admitted you liked!"

She turned to the drink she had neglected, and asked slowly and a little offhandedly, "What was the reason you took an interest in the phosphate mine? It belonged entirely to Cécile, didn't it?"

"Yes," he said, and left it there for a minute while he dropped more ice into his almost empty glass. Then, with a shrug that meant he might as well get it over, he stated, "I did take up the phosphate mine chiefly for Cécile's sake. She wasn't making much by her singing, and she told me that if she could sell the mine she would use the money to further her career. I engaged experts to investigate the mine, and it was discovered that with the expenditure of several thousand we could get it going again, on a profitable basis. I couldn't let Cécile sell out – it wouldn't have been fair."

"Why not?"

"Because she'd have lost money by it. It was only right to buy the mine as it stood and then form a company, of which she could own a proportion of the shares – and get her cut of the profits."

"Did she use the lump sum to further her career?"

He smiled faintly. "In a way I suppose she did. She bought expensive clothes galore, and assumed a veneer of success that brought in offers of contracts all over North Africa. Professionally, she was made."

"You two . . . stuck together, didn't you?"

He put down the glass and held her shoulders. "My dearest girl, you've spoiled me for every other woman in the world.

I used to enjoy Cécile – she was sophisticated and a good companion for the few weeks she used to stay in Shiran – but there was nothing more. I'm not blind, of course. She practically ignored other men, so I knew that some day she'd expect me to marry her. I hadn't much feeling about it, either way. I used to believe I wasn't the marrying kind – till you came."

"How are things now – with Cécile?"

"She's gone. Didn't you know?"

Sally lifted a wide blue glance. "No. I thought she had a few more days."

He plunged his hands back into his pockets. "I'd better explain. You know how I felt about that scene they arranged – Lucette's husband and the rest. I had the girl weeping over me, and after she was gone I was in a mood to do damage to someone. Well, first I saw Mike and told him he was leaving for England. Next day I had half an hour with Cécile; that was when I discovered that she'd been as deeply in it as Mike."

"You quarrelled with her?"

"Lord, no. We were painfully polite and nothing was openly discussed. I didn't leave her in doubt, though. I told her I thought she could give Le Perroquet a miss for a year or two, and reminded her that Shiran had no other night-club big enough to pay her fee. I also suggested that she looked too tired to complete her contract . . . you know, the old routine."

"What they call the charming brush-off?"

"That's right. It was she who suggested leaving Shiran today."

"She *is* beautiful," said Sally with a sigh.

"If you like honey-blondes. I don't. I go for a cross between chestnut and bronze and English colouring."

Sally smiled, but said soberly, "You did work insidiously and well on Cécile, didn't you? I believe I'm a bit afraid of you."

"Not you – you've got me in your pocket."

"You wouldn't say that so airily if it were true."

He grinned. "Don't get defensive again. It's just you and me now."

"But the mine still connects you with Cécile?"

"Oh, didn't I finish? I've offered to buy her out and I think she'll accept. It will be a sort of insurance for Mike, too. If he doesn't recover sufficiently to do his old job well, he'll get desperate. Any man needs independence, and if Mike owns a share in the mine and a directorship of sorts, he'll be able to please himself where he lives and do a spot of work when he feels like it."

"He hates your generosity, you know."

Dane lifted his shoulders and nodded. "It doesn't matter – he needs it. If he gets back into circulation I'll let up, and start demanding a few things from him. By the way, will you mind living at the villa till we find somewhere else?"

She pinked again. "Do we have to discuss that kind of thing so soon?"

"We could wait an hour, if you insist."

She smiled shakily. "I won't mind the villa . . . or any-where."

"Even the Mirador?"

"Well, I'd rather keep house, but . . . but I do like this hotel. It's where we met, and it's something you created."

"Tell you what – we'll occasionally spend a week here in this suite, and in the mornings you can sing right there, on the balcony, and I'll join in. I sing off-key, but you'll be too much in love to notice."

"Oh, Dane," she said huskily. "I'm so happy and relieved that you love me."

Which was the cue, of course, for him to repeat his assur-ances, very thoroughly. In his arms, Sally could only feel, she couldn't think. But when he released her, she thought of travelling to England with him, showing him off to the family, of the ceremony in the village church . . . and of Morocco again.

"Shall we always live here?" she asked, searching his face.

"Who knows, honey?" he said teasingly. "Is it important?"

"No, but I wouldn't like to lose touch with Shiran. I'm quite fond of Pierre."

"Don't mention Tony again or I'll get vicious!"

She chanced it. "I do think it was terribly hard to insist that he wait two years before he marries."

"What difference does it make? He hasn't even met the girl yet."

"But supposing he does find someone quite soon?"

"Even after that, it takes time."

"It didn't take *you* very long!"

Dane shoved an arm round her and hugged her. "We'll rescind the offending clause when we announce our engagement – tonight. Like royalty granting an amnesty to prisoners. Satisfied?"

"Very."

His tones lost distinctness. "I want you so much, Sally. I've waited all my life for this."

"We want each other," she murmured against his chin. "I love you more every minute."

His answer was lost in her hair, but it didn't matter. At last they were close, physically and spiritually. It wasn't important that she didn't yet fully understand this big masterful man who was to be her husband. They loved, and the understanding would come.

Further titles by Rosalind Brett
in our Classics series

35p net

Please turn to page 191 for further details

Also available this month in our
Classics series:

THE SILVER DOLPHIN
by Anne Weale

When nineteen-year-old Rachel Devon was left orphaned
and inexperienced on a lonely Caribbean island, she was
rescued by Niall Herrick, skipper of the yacht *Silver Dolphin*.
Niall thought he had found a solution to Rachel's problems
—but would it necessarily make her happy?

FULL TIDE
by Celine Conway

Peregrine's strange obsession to find the Elizabeth he had
known as a child annoyed the real Elizabeth, who was in
love with him. It annoyed her even more when another,
bogus Elizabeth appeared ready to fit in with his dreams.

VISIT TO ROWANBANK
by Flora Kidd

Margaret Dunne went to Rowanbank as a private nurse to
pull herself out of the doldrums, and all was well except the
insufferable Richard Morrell, who greeted her with the
words, 'Plain, wholesome, and oh! so good for us'!

35p

Available August 1976

Forthcoming Classics

TAMARISK BAY
by Kathryn Blair
Philip Brooke was a stranger to Jenny—she only knew that he seemed the sort who would know his mind and get his own way, and that he had a magnetism no woman could fail to notice. He had said that in a crowd they might not even notice each other—but what would happen when they were marooned together on the edge of the Sumatran jungle?

THE SOFT ANSWER
by Marjorie Moore
Sister Kay Somers had a strong character—but so had the distinguished surgeon, Peter Raynal. They seemed to be destined to come into conflict. Then disaster struck, and Kay lost her job at St. Jude's, *and* her fiancé Robin . . .

PRETENCE
by Roberta Leigh
It was while Ann was working at the Mellride Marriage Agency that the playwright Paul Mallison asked to be introduced to 'someone who's shy, rather plain and in her middle twenties' with a view to matrimony. It was only after Rosalie, the girl Ann chose, had fallen in love with Paul that Ann discovered that his application was not genuine—he was not seeking a wife but copy for his next play. Furious, Ann determined to revenge Rosalie. She never stopped to think that she might be playing with fire.

THE RANCHER NEEDS A WIFE
by Celine Conway
When Joanna took a vacation job in the backwoods, she unexpectedly found herself the only woman with three children, twenty cow-hands, several thousand cattle—and that overbearing rancher, Rafe Holford. Joanna pitied any girl who might try to cope with such a man, but when Helen Geyer appeared on the scene ready and willing to do just that, Joanna's feelings underwent a startling change!

35p net

Available September 1976